Sedulous

FIRST LADY SERIES
BOOK THREE

LACRICIA A'NGELLE

This book is a work of fiction. The characters, incidents, and dialogues are products of the author's imagination and are not to be construed as real. Any references to actual events, persons, living or dead, or to real locales are intended to give the novel a sense of reality.

Sedulous

Published by His Pen Publishing, LLC

Editor Shelia E. Bell

ISBN: 978-1-944643-17-1

Library of Congress Cataloging-in-Publication Data is available.

First Printing September 2023

This book is also available in digital eBook format.

Sedulous adjective

sed·u·lous ˈse-jə-ləs

: diligent in application or pursuit

Books by LaCricia A'ngelle

Girl, Naw!

It Ain't Over

Love Worth Fighting For Series

Journey to Love

Worthy of Love

First Lady Series

Positive Deception

Lina's Redemption

Sedulous

Stand Alone Books

Sophomore Mom

The Christmas Gift

No Christmas Without You

Coming Soon

Down By the Wishing Well

Thank you, Lord. Without you none of this would be possible.

This book is dedicated to my Family. I love you all.
Special thanks to my Mother Emma, my Husband Derwin,
my children and Editor Shelia E. Bell

One

"It's time to give God the praise!" The charismatic male voice boomed through the speakers of the seventy-inch television, filling the living room.

"Humph." Maxine picked up the remote and pressed the power button. It slipped from her fingers and landed on the couch with a slight thump. "Man, ain't nobody trying to hear you today, Pastor Lee." She spat out the name as if it was poison. "What a joke."

Maxine paced the length of the living room with folded arms. A light trail appeared on the carpet, marking the path her bare feet traveled.

How is his broadcast being shown on major networks anyway? Don't church shows only play on Christian networks and YouTube? He must be getting paid! She should have been the wife he was showering with accolades. It should've been her sitting in the special seat designated for the first lady of her ex-boyfriend's new mega church. Pastor Maxwell Lee had amassed millions through his speaking engagements and book sales. Now, here she was, standing on the outside looking in. Not that Maxine was interested in the whole church scene, but money was money, and she would take it any way she could get it. Legally, that is. Jail was not a place Maxine was interested in residing.

"Maybe I wasn't ready back then, but I could make it work now. Your loss, Maxwell," Maxine groaned. Moving over to the window, she pulled back the curtains. The view from her eighteenth-floor condo overlooking Navy Pier was breathtaking.

Maxine loved her place, but things between her and her boss, Jonathan Freeman, who was also her lover, had become strained. If their relationship ended, she didn't know how much longer she could keep up the mortgage payments. Jonathan's influence was the reason she still had her job, despite the office manager hating her. Even with Maxine's sixty-thousand-dollar savings, maintaining the lifestyle she'd become accustomed to would be a struggle.

She stepped away from the window and made her way to the kitchen. The cabinet door creaked as she reached inside and removed a wine glass. She filled her glass halfway and swirled the liquid inside. Maxine closed her eyes and inhaled the sensuous fragrance before turning her glass up to take a sip.

With the glass in one hand and bottle in the other, Maxine strolled over to the couch. A light tap echoed throughout the living room as she placed the wine bottle on the glass coffee table. Maxine took a seat and crossed her legs. She made a kicking movement and sipped wine as she calculated her next steps. Her cell phone buzzed in the pocket of the plush terry cloth robe that enveloped her body. She retrieved the phone and peered at the display that revealed her best friend's name and phone number.

"Hey, Rashi! What's up, chick?" Maxine's excitement was apparent in her tone.

"Girl, nothing. Just left the salon getting my hair done. I decided to try something new. I asked my stylist to put in twenty-seven-inch straight hair instead of the Brazilian wavy I always get."

"Okay, I'll bet it's cute on you."

"It's going to take some getting used to. With my caramel skin, I'm up here looking like a cartoon princess or something."

"Girl, you're a trip. I can't wait to see it. I don't remember the last time I saw you with straight hair."

"You don't have to wait. I already planned to do some shopping on Michigan Avenue today. Why don't you join me?"

"What time are you going?"

"In about an hour. I can swing by and get you if you feel up to going."

"Yeah, come by here. I need to get out. Otherwise, I'll end up drinking this entire bottle of wine."

"If you're drinking this early in the day, you shole need to get out of the house. I'll be there in a little while."

Maxine ended her call and placed the phone on the coffee table. She turned up her glass and downed the remnants of her drink. Sitting the glass on the table, she dashed into the bedroom to get ready.

The doorbell rang as Maxine applied the finishing touches to her makeup. She swept a layer of gloss on her lips and rubbed them together, ensuring an even application before heading to the door. She peered through the peephole to confirm her visitor's identity before pulling the door open.

"Hey, girl." Maxine pulled Rashida into an embrace. She stepped aside, making room for her friend to enter.

Rashida spied Maxine's bare feet and lack of jewelry. "Why aren't you ready?" Shaking her head, Rashida placed her purse on a small table near the front door and made her way into the space.

"I'm almost ready. Chill out." With a swift motion, Maxine lifted the ends of Rashida's hair and allowed it to fall around her shoulders. "Your hair is cute."

Running her fingers through the lengthy tresses, Rashida replied, "It's alright. I'll get used to it, I guess."

"Why did you get it so long with your miniature self? Girl, the hair literally comes down past your butt."

"That's alright. I'm highlighting my assets." Rashida stuck her tongue out while arching her back to make her butt appear bigger. "I'm trying to get one of those rich men, like you have. I know Jonathan has a friend he can introduce me to."

"Girl, please." Maxine stepped away from Rashida and retrieved her shoes from the bedroom. She returned within seconds hopping as she attempted to balance on one high heel shoe while putting on the other. "I might as well not have a man. Jonathan has been trippin' for real." Maxine stood firm, with both shoes in place. She grabbed her purse and keys. "I don't know what his problem is. Every time I turn around, he's blowing me off, talking about he has family obligations."

Raising an eyebrow, Rashida picked up her purse. "Well, the man is married. What are you going to do if he dips on you? I know this place and that car you drive is expensive."

"Jonathan paid for my car in full. I have the title, so I'm not worried about it. This condo is another story. The mortgage payment on this place is ridiculous. Although it's in my name, Jonathan makes the payments." Maxine pulled the front door open so she and Rashida could exit.

The ladies continued to chat on their way to Rashida's car. Winking, Maxine walked with an exaggerated sway, enticing the doorman and others in the lobby.

"Girl, you are too much," Rashida said, laughing.

"What?" Maxine replied, batting her eyes.

Maxine joined Rashida in laughter, heading to the car. Within minutes, the ladies were pulling into a parking garage on Michigan Avenue. Maxine loved living close to the famed shopping district. Having a condo in downtown Chicago was also convenient for her job.

"Let's get our shop on," Rashida exclaimed. "I need to get a few cute outfits and new lingerie for this weekend. One of my boos is taking me to Vegas."

"Why Vegas?" Maxine asked, turning up her lip.

"Because he's a high roller, and he loves to gamble. Don't be turning your lips up. I gets mine, believe that."

Maxine raised her palms and shook her head. "My bad. Trust me, girlfriend, if you like it, I love it. I've been to Vegas. There's a lot to do, but if your man likes to gamble, you'll get bored. Unless, of course, you like to do things by yourself."

"How is it possible that even your apology sounds petty? Girl, you're a trip."

"Stop being so sensitive." Maxine pulled on Rashida's arm, guiding her into the department store. "Come on, let's go in Saks."

Once inside the store, the ladies made their way to the shoe department. They both loved shoes. Rashida picked up a pair of strappy hot pink sandals. She held them up and asked the salesclerk to get her a size eight.

"Those are cute," Maxine acknowledged. "You better be glad you saw them before I did."

"They're a little less than seven hundred. That's a steal. You should get a pair. They even come in black."

"That's alright. You go ahead. We can't be walking around here twinning."

Maxine scanned the walls and picked up a Jimmy Choo crystal glitter sandal. An eager salesclerk approached her when she saw Maxine showing interest in the shoe.

"Would you like to try those on?" the woman, who appeared to be just over the age of eighteen, asked.

"Yes, I'll take a size ten if you have it."

The clerk smiled and hurried to the back room.

Maxine and Rashida modeled their selections for each other before completing their purchases and moving on to the next store. The ladies continued shopping for a few hours before taking a break for lunch at Lafayette Cafe.

"So, girl, what's up with you and Jonathan? You've been making slick comments about him all day. Sounds like trouble in paradise."

"I wouldn't go that far. We're doing okay, but Jonathan has been trippin' a lot. He's blown me off more times than I want to deal with. To be honest, I'm tired of the whole other woman thing. I require too much attention to be a side chick. I might even consider being wifey if the right man made it worth my while."

"Too bad things didn't work out with you and Maxwell. It seems like I see him every time I logon to my social media accounts. If it's not a live broadcast, it's an ad. He must be pulling in money left and right. All that advertising has to be expensive." Rashida bit into her kale veggie burger and swirled a French fry in ketchup.

"Please. Don't even mention that punk. I can't stand him." Maxine took a sip of water to push the remnants of her food down. "Now," she continued. "I will say, being with a preacher might not be a bad idea. Those bad boys be getting money hand over fist. Shoot, I'm going to do just that."

"What?"

"I'm going to find me a preacher. Since most of the popular preachers all seem to have wives, I'm going to find one that's on the come up. I'll fix him up, then cash in on my investment." Maxine stabbed a forkful of baked ziti and put it in her mouth.

"You're crazy. First of all, where are you going to find a man like that?"

"At one of those church conventions they're always having. Haven't you seen the advertisements? They have billboards and everything. Those things be loaded with preachers and regular men. I might get lucky and end up with a two for one deal."

Rashida burst into laughter. She stopped long enough to take a sip of red wine. Rashida soon realized Maxine was not laughing along with her. Lowering her glass, she stared at her friend. "You're serious."

"Yes, I'm serious. I wouldn't joke about something like that."

"I'm sorry. I can't see it happening. You're my girl, so I won't lie to you. You are way too bougie to pull it off. I mean, let's be real. What if you find a guy that fits into your plan, but he's ugly? Would you still go through with it?"

Maxine pushed the food around on her plate. "Honey, I am sedulous. I don't stop until I get what I want." Maxine pointed her fork in Rashida's direction to emphasize her point. "Huh, I can put up with more than you think. I've kissed a lot of frogs in my day. If the man is worth it, I will make it happen."

"There's no way you just came up with this idea. I know you, Maxine. You've been thinking about this for a while."

"Yeah, I have. It started when I dated Maxwell. The way people were pawning over the preachers and their wives was cool."

"I know what you're talking about. Believe it or not, I was raised in church. I think we were there every time the door was open. That's why I don't go to church now. It was church overload. You're right about one thing, though. People would fall over themselves trying to do stuff for the pastor and his wife. They treated them like they were straight up celebrities."

"Exactly."

Rashida took another sip from her glass and peered at Maxine. The glass still resting on her lip. "I don't know how you can do it. What if the dude is unattractive? Because if he's fine, with the way things are these days, either he's already taken or he's playing for the other team."

"I can handle it as long as he's a fixer upper that's worth it. He has to have some potential."

"I can't wait to see how this turns out." Rashida raised her glass and stretched her arm toward Maxine. "A toast to your future husband."

Maxine raised her glass and tapped it against Rashida's. "Cheers. Let the hunt begin."

"Yes, girlfriend. If you're going to do this, you gotta do it right. Let's get out of here and buy you some church hats."

"That's what I'm talking about. Let's do this." Maxine turned up her glass and downed the remnants of her drink. She beckoned the server over and paid the bill. They made their way to the exit with a clear mission.

"Maxine," a male voice called out, stopping her in her tracks.

Two

The man held the door open and allowed Maxine and Rashida to exit the restaurant. Once they were all outside, he pulled Maxine into a gentle embrace.

"How are you doing?" he asked, stepping back to take in the full view of her. "I haven't seen you in a while. What have you been up to?"

"I'm good. Just out here doing a little shopping. Nothing new on my end. How about you?"

Rashida looked back and forth between Maxine and the man that she'd yet to be introduced to. She cleared her throat, gaining their attention.

Maxine spoke first. "My bad, girl," she said, looking at Rashida. "Jason, this is my friend, Rashida. Rashida, this is Jason. He's a friend from back in the day. We sort of grew up together."

"Yeah, until she moved away," he interjected. "I thought Maxine was going to be my sister-in-law, as crazy as she was about my brother."

"It was not that deep. We were friends. Just like you and me."

"Ah, okay. If you say so. I thought it was more than that, but it's all good. You're looking as fine as ever, and he's doing good too. I guess everything worked out the way it was supposed to."

"Indeed, it did." Maxine looked at her watch and then at Rashida before returning her gaze to Jason. "It was good seeing you. I hate to rush off, but me and my girl are on a mission."

Stepping closer, he gave Maxine a quick hug and winked at Rashida. "It was good seeing you, Maxine. Nice to meet you, Rashida. You ladies have a good day."

Without another word, Maxine and Rashida walked away, toward Nordstrom.

"What was that all about?" Rashida asked. "Who is this brother he thought you were going to marry?"

"Jason is Maxwell's brother. I guess you can say he reunited Maxwell and me. I saw him one day at Walgreen's. We hadn't seen each other in years. I told him to have Maxwell call me, and the rest is pretty much history. Humph, I didn't need him telling me how good Maxwell is doing."

"Hold up. You're not getting off that easy. Talking about the rest is history. You never gave me the full details of what happened between you and Maxwell. All I remember is you saying you were focusing your attention on Jonathan. You said Maxwell wasn't worth your time."

Maxine browsed the clothing rack, sliding the garments from one end to the next. "I wasn't interested in Maxwell to begin with. He was alright, but I didn't want anything serious. Jonathan was, and still is, taking excellent care of me. I knew Maxwell couldn't come up to that level."

She removed a dress from the rack and held it up, examining it. "Truth is, I was using him to cover up my affair with Jonathan. It was going good until my mama opened her big mouth and told his mother some stuff about me. Maxwell came to my job and cold busted me. Jonathan was having gifts delivered to me anonymously. I told everyone in the office they were from Maxwell. So, when Maxwell showed up, one of my co-workers complimented him on the gifts. He had the nerve to take me outside and tried to check me. You know I wasn't going for that. By the time I finished getting him together, it was a wrap."

Engrossed in Maxine's story, Rashida asked, "What happened next? Knowing you the way I do, I'm sure you didn't let things end like that."

"You know what, I did. I haven't talked to or seen him since. As much as he's dominating social media and local television stations, it's hard not to see him and that church of his. Who knew the brother would come up?" Maxine grabbed a few dresses from the rack. "I'm going to try these on. I'll be back."

Maxine stepped out of the dressing room wearing a fitted one shoulder white dress that fell just below the knee. She glanced around for Rashida when she was distracted by a man raising his voice at the salesclerk. Maxine stood in front of the mirror, pretending to assess her appearance while listening to the exchange.

"Why is there an issue with me returning this suit? I have the receipt right here." The frustrated man held the receipt up to the clerk.

"I understand that sir. However, this is a gift receipt. We cannot give cash back with a gift receipt. You're welcome to browse the store and exchange the item for something of equal value. Otherwise, we can credit back the card the person used to purchase this suit."

"There isn't a thing in this store I want."

"In that case, sir, the only other option I can offer is to issue you a gift card for the amount of the return."

"What am I supposed to do with a gift card?" he barked. "I just said..."

Maxine turned away from the mirror at the exact moment the man looked up. She looked at the worn Chicago Bulls t-shirt and denim jeans he was wearing and wondered why he wasn't interested in the suit. He wasn't an ugly man, a little on the hefty side, but fixable. Their eyes met, and she diverted her attention.

"I tell you what," the man continued talking to the clerk with an elevated tone. "Give me the gift card."

"Yes, sir." The clerk completed the transaction and handed the card over to the man. Relief displayed on her face as he stepped away.

From the mirror's reflection, Maxine could see the man approaching her. She swallowed the lump trying to form in her throat.

"That dress is beautiful on you," the man said, scanning Maxine from head to toe. "You should get it."

Maxine opened her mouth to say thank you.

"In fact," he interrupted and stretched out his hand, presenting her with the gift card. "Use this to pay for it and whatever else the money on this card will buy."

Shock registered on Maxine's face. "Are you serious?"

"Very serious. Enjoy the rest of your day. God bless you."

"Thank you," Maxine replied, watching the man walk away.

Rashida came running up to Maxine after the man stepped away. She had been watching from a short distance. "Girl, what just happened? Do you know him?"

"No. I've never seen him in my life. I'm sitting here trying to figure it out."

"Um hmm, you sitting up here looking good in that dress and you got strangers walking up giving you money. Had I not seen it happen for myself, I would swear up and down you were lying. I guess there's no question. You better get this dress."

Maxine sashayed around in a circle, swinging her hips. "Honey, trust and believe it's not the dress. It's the body underneath the dress. Don't get it twisted."

"Ugh, get in there and try on those other dresses so we can go. I don't have all day to be fooling with you." Rashida gave Maxine a soft push, directing her toward the dressing room.

After finalizing her selections, Maxine made her way to the checkout. She was interested to see how much the gift card was worth. She was prepared to pay the full amount for her purchases, but having the gift card would free her money up for other stuff.

The cash register beeped as the clerk scanned her items. "Your total is $527.15."

Maxine reached inside her purse, fished out her wallet, and retrieved both the gift card she received from the stranger and her credit card. She handed the gift card to the salesclerk first.

"I'm not sure how much is on this card," she said. "Apply whatever is on here to the total and then I'll put the balance on my credit card."

"No problem." The clerk pointed to the card reader on the counter and instructed Maxine to slide the gift card. The receipt printer buzzed as it eased out the printed slip of paper. Smiling, the clerk tore off the receipt, handed it to Maxine, and bagged her items.

"That's it? You don't need my credit card?"

"No. There were enough funds on the card to cover it." She pulled the receipt back from Maxine and circled the card balance. "If you look here, you will see there's $388.28 remaining on the card."

Maxine's mouth fell open. "Are you serious?"

The clerk smiled and handed Maxine her purchase.

Joining Rashida, the ladies squealed in delight at the unexpected news.

"I guess that's your sign, Maxine. The only thing left is for you to get your man."

"Correction, the thing we need to do now is figure out what you're going to wear, because you're coming too."

"What?"

Three

THE CAR SHOOK FROM THE IMPACT OF RASHIDA slamming the door shut. She adjusted her skirt and marched around to the driver's side to meet Maxine. "I can't believe you made me come with you. There are some things that even I won't do. You and I both know I will try just about anything, but I draw the line at playing with God."

"Stop being so dramatic, Rashi. It's church. We're here to praise the Lord." Maxine waved a gloved hand in the air. "If we happen to find a man in the process of our praise, then it'll be a blessing from the Lord." Her shoulders rose, touching her earrings. "I don't know a lot of scriptures, but I know God brought Eve to Adam. The same way He brought me here today to find my man. Now, stop stalling and let's get inside. I want to be in there while everyone is still mingling."

Maxine retrieved an oversized black and white hat from the back seat and placed it on her head, using her car window as a mirror. She rubbed her tongue across her teeth to remove the splotch of lipstick that had settled on a front tooth.

Maxine sashayed into the church with Rashida trailing close

behind. Her white form fitting knee-length dress with a split on the left thigh, along with four-inch black and white Christian Louboutin heels tapped on the polished concrete floor, drawing immediate attention. Maxine arched her back, forcing her size D breasts out further. She smirked at the hat wearing women that snubbed her and grabbed the arm of their husbands as she and Rashida made their way through the crowd.

"That right there will never be me," Maxine said to Rashida, using her eyes to point toward a group of women wearing long dresses with necklines up to their chin. "I'm gonna keep it classy and cute. Some of these women look half dead, stressed, and depressed."

"I hope you know what you're getting yourself into. From what I hear, being a first lady ain't no joke. Those women look stressed for a reason."

Maxine waved her hand, dismissing Rashida. "That depends on the woman. A strong woman knows how to exercise her power to get what she wants from her husband or anyone else."

Rashida was growing tired of Maxine's arrogance. Maxine had an answer for everything, even when she didn't have a clue about the subject. The two had been friends for several years and pulled a lot of schemes together. Most of which Rashida was in full agreement. This whole *bag a preacher* scheme was beyond Rashida's comfort zone. She would allow Maxine to feel like she was on her side, but in reality, she was waiting for her friend to fall flat on her face.

Music flowed from the sanctuary, beckoning the crowds inside. The congregants moved in droves, filling the massive space.

"We better get inside," Rashida said.

Maxine moved in the opposite direction, heading toward the ladies' room. She sighed in frustration. "Haven't I taught you anything? Lord, you act like you just met me." She stepped inside the restroom and stood in front of the mirror. Smoothing down the sides of her dress, she turned, examining her butt.

"You don't rush in when everyone else goes in. Wait until everyone is seated, then let the ushers escort you to a seat." Maxine pulled out her compact and powdered her nose. "The key is to make sure they put you near the front so more people see you."

Rashida tugged on the ends of her hair and bit her lip to keep from telling Maxine her true feelings. After watching Maxine primp for ten minutes, Rashida had enough. "Are you ready to go yet? It's getting a little raunchy in here." She looked toward a woman changing a baby's putrid diaper.

Covering her nose, Maxine removed her small handbag from the sink and headed toward the exit. As predicted, the usher escorted the ladies to seats near the front of the church. Maxine scoped out the area as she passed by. She and Rashida scooted into the row and claimed two empty seats. Maxine squealed in delight as she whispered in Rashida's ear, pointing out the section filled with men dressed in black suits and cleric collars. She noticed several of the men looking in her direction. Maxine smiled and gave a slight nod.

"Hey, Maxine," Rashida leaned over and whispered, "Isn't that the guy that gave you the gift card sitting over there with the preachers?"

"Where?" Maxine asked, scanning the group.

"Third row, fifth from the left."

"Ooh, that is him," Maxine acknowledged. "Do you think he saw us?"

"How could he not?" Rashida replied with a slight grin. *Everybody saw you with that spectacle you made of yourself.* Rashida thought.

The service continued despite Maxine's constant attempts at drawing attention to herself. She did everything from jumping up and swaying to the music before the choir started singing, to finding a bogus reason to linger at the offering basket.

When the service ended, Maxine reminded Rashida to inch toward the exit doors. She was certain she had multiple admirers and didn't want to risk missing out on meeting her future husband. Rashida rolled her eyes in protest but complied with her friend's request.

The ladies lingered in the vestibule as the attendees made their way to the exit. Rashida noticed several of the men who sat among the ministers shuffle through the crowd, smiling and shaking hands with parishioners. A man with smooth skin the shade of polished oak approached them, causing Rashida to choke on her own spit.

She turned away from the man and spoke to Maxine in a low tone. "Girl, that man is fine. He looks so good he makes me want to climb that tree he calls a body and devour the forbidden fruit. Lord have mercy, I didn't know they still came that fine." Easing back around, Rashida inhaled, filling her lungs with the essence of his cologne as she scanned him from the wavy jet-black hair on his head to the Mezlan alligator shoes on his feet. His sexy brown eyes framed with thick black brows captivated her. He offered an infectious smile, revealing embedded dimples.

"Hello, ladies. I don't believe we've met. My name is Pastor Alvin Adams." He extended his hand to Maxine for a handshake.

"Nice to meet you, Pastor Adams," Maxine said, giving him a quick handshake before shifting his attention from her over to Rashida. "This is my friend, Rashida. Perhaps the two of you could get to know each other. Excuse me for a moment, please."

Maxine left Rashida and Alvin together. She spotted the guy from the mall standing with two other men and headed in his direction. Standing behind him, she tapped him on the shoulder, gaining his attention.

"Excuse me," she said as he turned in her direction.

His companions looked at each other, astonished at the beautiful woman's interest in their friend. Without a word exchanged, they looked at each other and walked away, leaving Maxine and the minister alone.

Eli couldn't mask his surprise at seeing the gorgeous woman from the department store. He scanned her body. A slight smile creased his lips. "Hello. What a pleasure it is to see you again."

"Thank you. It surprised me to see you sitting with the ministers today. You were pretty upset that day at the store. I never would have imagined you were a minister."

"I'm sorry your first encounter with me was during an unfavorable moment. As you know, I was less than pleased with the way they handled my return. At the time I didn't understand it, but seeing you in this dress, I know I made the right decision giving you the gift card. In my mind, I was being a blessing to a random stranger. I didn't expect to see you again, especially at church."

"What do you mean, especially at church? You don't know me well enough to make a statement like that. In fact, you don't know me at all." Maxine was rethinking her decision to approach the man whose name she still didn't know. Who was he to judge her? For all he knew, she could have been a regular church attendee. Apparently, he was basing his assessment solely on her appearance, like many people had.

Eli extended his right hand. "You're right. I can admit when I'm wrong. By the way, my name is Jasper Clayton, but you can call me Eli. Those that are close to me know that's the name I prefer."

"Why Eli?"

"Jasper is a family name. I got it by default, being the oldest grandson. My middle name is Elijah, which I consider restrictive, especially with Elijah being a prophet in the Bible. However, Eli fits. I can be myself without having to fit into a pre-designed mold."

Maxine wrapped her hand around his. "I'm Maxine Miller. It's nice to formally meet you, Eli."

"We've met twice now at random. It must be a sign. Perhaps you will allow me to take you to dinner."

"I see you're a man who doesn't appear to believe in taking things slow."

Eli rubbed his chin and shrugged. "I can see why you would think that. I believe when you see something you want and the conditions are favorable, you go for it. No need to delay the obvious. I might as well shoot my shot, as they say."

"How do you know you want me? You've seen me twice. This is the first time you've ever had a conversation with me."

"Then let me take you to dinner and I can show you what I already believe to be true."

"I could do that, but it would be too easy." Maxine placed a hand on her hip and touched her bottom lip with the index finger on her right hand. She paused a moment as she considered Eli's offer.

"Tell you what, since we've had two unexpected encounters, I'm inclined to believe the third time's the charm. I'll agree to go to dinner with you, but only if we have one more surprise encounter. Don't even think about stalking me. It needs to be random like these other times. If it happens, we'll both know our meeting was no coincidence."

Laughing, Eli shook his head. "You're kidding, right?"

"Nope, I'm dead serious." Maxine extended her hand to Eli. "Can we shake on it?"

"It sounds like I don't have a choice." Eli took Maxine's hand in his. "You have a deal. With that, I will bid you ado until we meet again."

"I look forward to it." Maxine offered a slight smile before turning and heading back in Rashida's direction.

Rashida wrote her phone number on a piece of paper and pressed it into Alvin's hand. She tried to be discrete not wanting to garner too much attention from the church attendees. "I hope to hear from you soon, Pastor Adams," she breathed.

Maxine cleared her throat, catching Rashida off guard. "I hate to break up what seems to be a wonderful conversation, but we need to go Rashida... now."

"Girl, I know you're trippin," Rashida said with a bite in her tone. Alvin stepped away, avoiding unnecessary conflict.

Looping her arm around a resistant Rashida, Maxine pulled her toward the exit.

Four

"GET YOUR HAND OFF ME." RASHIDA JERKED HER ARM out of Maxine's grasp once they were outside the church. "What you did was not cool. I know you saw me talking to Alvin. I'm getting real tired of your crap. Don't make me lay hands on you at this church."

"Girl, calm down. I did you a favor."

"What do you mean? Do you think you're the only one who can have a man that fine interested in her?"

Maxine continued walking to the car, ignoring Rashida's rant. Once they were secure inside, she started the car and drove away from the church's lot.

"I'm not playing with you, Maxine. You went too far this time. You need to give me the same respect I give you. I didn't say anything when you were talking to that bald, chunky man. He must be rich because he looked a mess with all those blemishes on his face and that hotdog roll behind his head."

"Eli didn't look that bad. Since you want to dwell on looks, I pulled you away from what's his name."

"Alvin. His name is Alvin," Rashida interjected.

"Alvin, Simon, Theodore, it doesn't matter. He is too fine. Trust me. You don't want a man that fine. If he's not conceited, which he probably is, then you'll spend all your time fighting off other women. The man is so fine he makes you want to walk up and lick him."

Rashida turned to Maxine and burst into laughter. "Don't be trying to make me laugh. I'm mad at you."

"You know it's true. That's why you're laughing. I thought I would have to put a bib on you as much as you were drooling."

"Shut up. I'm laughing because you're crazy. I don't know how you come up with some of the stuff you say. You're trying to change the subject or distract me. I'm still upset. How you handled the situation was not cool. You need to realize I'm your friend, not your child."

"I know, munchkin. You're just so tiny, sometimes I forget you're a grown woman." Maxine moved to pinch Rashida's cheek, but halted when Rashida smacked her hand away.

"You better not touch my face."

Maxine pulled up to Rashida's apartment building and parked next to the curb. She moved the gearshift into the park position. As the car idled, Maxine turned to Rashida with a serious expression. "Look, I ain't trying to tell you what to do. Your life is your life. I'm not trying to be your mama. I've been in the game a lot longer than you, so I've learned a few things. If you like that Alvin guy, then go for it. Just don't make it a love thing. Shake that thang, collect some change, and move on. Trust me on this, anything more will be trouble."

"Look, Maxine. I appreciate your advice and insight or whatnot, but I know how to behave myself. I got this." Rashida pulled on the handle and pushed the door open. She placed her right foot on the curb and moved to exit but turned back. "Tell me something. What was up with that chubby bald guy you were pushing up on? I know he gave you the gift card and all, but I don't see how you can have any genuine interest in him. At least Alvin is fine."

"Sometimes it's not about what you see in the beginning. He seems like a nice guy. Besides, I can turn a frog into a prince if he's worth it. Like I was trying to tell you before you got all defensive, look beyond the moment and see the long term. The chubby guy, as you call him, is an investment who will pay out handsomely."

"Whatever you say. In the end, we'll find out who was right about both guys." Rashida stepped out of the vehicle and pushed the door closed. Although she'd put up with a lot of Maxine's cockiness, it wasn't bad enough for her to sever ties.

Maxine pulled away from the curb and sped down the street. When it came to dating, she was normally more particular about the men she gave her time and attention to, but her priorities had changed. If she was going to become a first lady, she might have to make some concessions. If that meant lending her time and attention to an unattractive man, then so be it. Besides, no one said she would have to be faithful to the guy. He would serve one purpose. Anything she wanted beyond being his wife for the first lady perks she could get from more desirable suitors.

She pressed the Power button on the radio. Maxine snapped her fingers and swayed to the soulful sounds of Jill Scott's "Golden." It was an older song, but it described her to a T. She sang above the melody, feeling the music like warm blood rushing through her veins. Maxine reached the peak of the song when the music came to an abrupt stop, replaced by the ringing of an incoming call. Recognizing the familiar number displayed on the dashboard, she pressed the Accept key.

"Hello, handsome," she said in a sultry tone. "How did you know I was thinking of you?"

"I'll bet you were. Where were you? I've been trying to reach you."

"I was in church," Maxine stammered.

"Since when do you attend church? As long as I've known you, church has not been a part of your life, so are you going to tell me the truth or keep lying?"

"Jonathan, I'm not lying. I was in church. I went with Rashida."

Maxine hated when Jonathan tried to intimidate her. She'd often heard older men dating younger women had what people considered *daddy* issues. Often, they couldn't distinguish between a girlfriend and a child, but this was ridiculous. Especially since she had, in fact, been in church. Realizing there was no sense in trying to change his mind, Maxine changed the subject.

"What's going on with you, baby? If you can get away, I'd love for you to drop by. Come over and let me show you how much I've missed you."

"I came by earlier. You weren't home. Allison has plans for us this evening, so getting away is out of the question. Had I known you were going to pull a disappearing act, I wouldn't have wasted my time coming over there today."

"Baby, I'm sorry. Rashida asked me to go to church with her and I said yes. I hadn't talked to you in several days. There was no way I could forewarn you. I figured you were out of town or something. Perhaps things will work out and you can come by later tonight. Either way, I'll be home, ready and waiting."

"Don't bother. I told you I have plans with my wife. If you had been home like you were supposed to be, we wouldn't be having this conversation right now."

Jonathan raised his voice, setting Maxine on edge. She hated his controlling nature. If she didn't make him aware of her exact whereabouts, he threw a fit. When he got furious, he would cut her off financially.

"I'm sorry, baby. Maybe I'll get to see you at the office

tomorrow. We can have one of our special meetings." Maxine's sultry tone oozed seduction.

"Yeah, whatever. You just make sure the next time I call you answer. I put too much money into you to deal with trying to chase you down."

Maxine gasped. Throughout their relationship, Jonathan had alluded to the amount of money he spent on her. Not to mention the cash he gave her. Never had he come right out and compared her to a house or vehicle he fixed up. She was trying to hold on to Jonathan until she put her new plan in place, but he was making it almost unbearable. As bad as she wanted to respond, Maxine knew her response would do more harm than good.

Jonathan's statement served as further confirmation to Maxine that it was time to move on. Her mind drifted to Eli Clayton. She knew she was taking a risk in showing interest in him. Especially since she had no way of knowing if he could take care of her. Maxine was so caught up in her thoughts about Eli that she forgot Jonathan was on the phone. Music blared through the speakers, showing the call had ended.

"Now he's going to be pissed big time," Maxine said aloud, rolling her eyes in frustration. Things needed to change, sooner rather than later.

Five

Eli sat behind his large cherry wood desk and thought about the woman that captivated him. It had been two weeks since he last saw her, but he couldn't get Maxine out of his mind. Pushing his chair back, he stood and walked over to the window overlooking his massive car dealership. His heart swelled with pride as he watched the sales staff interact with customers. Eli still found it hard to believe he was the owner of such a thriving dealership.

He thanked God daily for his father, Noah, who made his dream of owning a dealership a reality by gifting Eli and his brother each with fifty million dollars. Even after giving such large amounts to the brothers, his parents were set for the rest of their lives with the remaining one hundred and fifty-eight million they had from their lottery win.

Eli was careful to keep his wealth quiet. He knew he wasn't the most attractive man there was. His receding hairline and two hundred eighty pounds, five foot eleven inch frame made him less than desirable. No matter how hard he tried, he couldn't seem to maintain the weight loss he achieved many times in the past.

Only close family members, and his best friend Zachariah, knew his financial status. Eli maintained a modest lifestyle. When asked about his employment, he told people he worked at the car dealership in a management position. They did not know he was the owner. Eli wondered what Maxine's motive was for approaching him. There was no way she could have known the details of his life. Their meeting at the department store had been random. Seeing each other at church had been purely coincidental. Hadn't it?

Never in his thirty-eight years of life had a woman as beautiful as Maxine Miller shown interest in him. His mind drifted back to the first time he laid eyes on her. The look of surprise when he'd given her the gift card. Recalling the amount, he smacked his head with the palm of his hand. *I am such an idiot.* Of course, she would show an interest in him. He had given her a thousand dollar gift card. He figured she assumed he was wealthy. Otherwise, why would a man dressed in a ratty t-shirt and jeans give away a gift card valued so high? Disappointment settled in as he dismissed the idea of becoming involved with Maxine.

Eli allowed himself to fantasize about what life would be like to have a woman like Maxine by his side. Following their conversation at the church, his fellow ministers swarmed him, both married and single, desperate to know his involvement with the woman whose body looked as if the hands of an expert sculpted it. Not knowing where things would lead between him and Maxine, Eli let the men use their imaginations.

"Mr. Clayton, your father is on line one," Eli's receptionist announced through the phone's intercom.

"Thank you. Please put him through."

The phone buzzed once before Eli lifted the receiver from its base.

"Hey, Dad, what's going on? Why didn't you call my cell phone?"

"Because I didn't want to. I enjoy calling you at work. It feels good knowing you made a wise investment with the money we gave you. Now, that brother of yours is a different story. Why he felt the need to have mansions in New York, Los Angeles, and Orlando is beyond me. It's not like he can lay his head in more than one place at a time. Between those cars and motorcycles of his, he 'bout has more vehicles than you have on your car lot." Mr. Clayton let out an exasperated sigh. "For the life of me, I can't figure out why he felt the need to buy a darn private island in the Bahamas. He spent fifteen million on that thing alone. I swear, that boy is going to send me to a premature grave and if he does, he can forget it because he won't get another dime. See, you're different, you're more like me. That's why I bought you that expensive boat, even though I had already given you money. You're so much more responsible than that brother of yours..."

"Dad, relax. You know how Brennon is. He's been a flashy guy since we were kids. His actions shouldn't surprise you. I'm sure he's not blowing all his money. At least I hope he's not." Eli relaxed in his chair and tapped his forehead with the phone receiver. He grew tired of having the same conversation with his father. It didn't matter if they were on the phone or in person, his brother always ended up being the topic of conversation.

"I sure hope you're right, son. Especially since he has all those kids."

"He has three children. Only one more than you and Mom." Eli was certain his frustration had become clear.

"I know how many grandbabies I got. I also know they daddy ain't gone act right. That's why me and ya mama put a little something back for them. Got em' all a trust fund at the bank. We'll do the same for your kids, if you ever decide to have any."

There you have it, Eli thought. He knew it would only be a matter of time before his father started in on him. Fortunately,

Noah had called him at the dealership, giving him an excuse to end the call.

"Hey, Dad, I hate to cut you off, but I have to get back to work."

"What do you mean? You're the boss," Mr. Clayton protested.

"Yes, I know. Which is why I must set the example for my staff. Besides, I have some pressing issues I need to tend to."

"Alright then, I'll let you go. I expect to see you over this way sometime soon."

Relieved, he exhaled. "You will. Make sure you kiss Mom for me."

Mr. Clayton ended the call without saying goodbye. Eli was used to his father's habit of ending calls and visits without the common valediction. Growing up in the Clayton household, his father had been adamant about instilling this into his sons. He told them goodbye was too final, therefore forbidding them from saying goodbye to him or their friends and family.

Eli exhaled, exaggerating the action. As much as he desired to go back to business as usual, he couldn't keep his mind off Maxine. The thought of having a woman like her on his arm was intriguing. A smile creased his lips as he allowed his mind to drift into depths he wished even God wouldn't see.

The buzzing of the cell phone on his belt startled him, shaking him from his thoughts. He sat up straight, drawing a cross with his hands from his head to his chest. "Lord, forgive me," he whispered. Looking down at his hand, he shook his head and chuckled. "What am I doing? I'm not Catholic." The phone continued to buzz.

Pulling the phone from its holder, Eli glanced at the screen before answering. "Good morning, Pastor Scott," Eli answered in a jovial tone. "How's it going?"

"Good morning, Elder. Everything's good," Pastor Scott

replied, matching his tone. “I’m calling about our twelve o’clock meeting. If you don’t mind, I’d like to meet at Chicago Cut. I skipped breakfast this morning, so I figured since we’re meeting anyway, we might as well grab lunch while we’re at it.”

“Yeah, Pastor. I can do that.”

“Alright, Doc. I guess I’ll see you in a little while.”

“Sure thing.” Eli ended the call. Though he dared not let it show during his phone call, his pastor’s desire to go to Chicago Cut perturbed him. The world-famous steakhouse was one of the more expensive restaurants in the city. His pastor would never ask Eli to cover the cost of his meal. Instead, he would request the meals be placed on one check and slowly reach for his wallet while Eli offered to pay. Eli went along with the pathetic charade out of respect for his pastor’s position.

Pastor Scott was one of the few people that knew about the sizable sum of money Eli received from his parents. Being a faithful tither, it seemed natural for him to pay tithes to his place of worship. When he put the cashier’s check in the donation box, the trustees alerted the pastor. Soon after, Pastor Scott started treating Eli like they were best friends. Their church comprised a little over five hundred members, including at least twenty members of the ministerial staff. The obvious favoritism didn’t go over well with some ministers, but they dared not challenge Pastor Scott.

Within a few months of his donation, Pastor Scott added Eli to the board of trustees and offered him more opportunities to deliver the Sunday morning message. Eli knew it was because of his financial contribution, but he didn’t let it discourage him. God had called him to ministry, and he was determined to walk in that calling.

Light taps on the door distracted him from the arduous task of balancing the dealership’s quarterly operating budget. Looking up, he acknowledged Hector Rodriguez, his sales manager, and beckoned him inside.

"Hector, my man, how's it going?"

"Everything's good, Mr. Clayton. The sales staff is raving about the competition you put in place. They're working hard to win the weekend getaway at the Palmer House Hotel. I'll tell you, I wish I was eligible to take part. You're offering a sweet deal."

"I'm glad the competition is going over well. You know I'm a firm believer, if you treat your people well, they will reciprocate. I like to put myself in their position when I decide on our quarterly competition. As you know, before I purchased this dealership, I went through the ranks. Starting as a salesman. With a lot of hard work and determination, I was promoted to general manager. When I was in sales, I would have loved an all-expenses paid weekend getaway in a suite, along with the use of a company car."

"You and me both, sir." Hector adjusted himself in the chocolate brown leather chair opposite Eli's desk. "Your girl, Bridgette, is killing it. She's running circles around the vets. She just completed the deal on her tenth vehicle. Bridgette achieved that in the last three days she's worked. She sold four on both Friday and Saturday, and another two this morning. It's not even noon. I'm telling you, she'll be coming for my job before long."

Eli folded his hands, touching his index fingers together. "That's my girl. I knew she'd be great. All throughout school Bridgette won top prizes for every school fundraiser she took part in." Laughing at the thought, Eli continued, "I ended up with more cookies, candy, and junk I didn't need than I care to admit. When her dad approached me at church and told me she was interested in selling cars, I didn't hesitate to bring her on board."

"You made an excellent choice. Now if I can just get the others to do the same, we'll have a record-breaking quarter."

"You've always done an outstanding job of motivating the team and driving our sales forward. I have complete faith you will continue to do so, Hector. I appreciate all you do for this dealership. Your efforts don't go unnoticed."

"Thank you, Mr. Clayton. I love my job. It doesn't feel like work. Besides, it gets me out of the house. If I had to spend all day with my wife and her mother, I'd be loco." The men shared a hearty laugh before turning their attention to the day's sales projections.

Six

Eli steered his SUV through the busy downtown traffic, stopping in front of the restaurant. He pushed his gearshift into the park position and smiled at the valet as he opened the door. Eli shook his hand, concealing a generous tip. The young man's smile widened when he recognized the familiar texture in his hand. Eli stepped around the vehicle and made his way to the entrance of the restaurant.

Holding the door open, Eli stepped aside, allowing a small group of women to exit. The women offered him thanks while continuing their conversations and laughter. Noticeable shock registered on his face when he recognized the beautiful woman approaching him.

Maxine locked eyes with Eli. Separating herself from her party, she stepped aside, pulling him away from the door. "What are you doing here?" she asked. The elevated pitch revealed her obvious frustration. "Are you stalking me or something?"

Furrowing his eyebrows, Eli widened his stance. "No. As much as I hate to disappoint you, I'm not stalking you. I'm meeting someone for lunch." He pulled his cell phone from his pocket. "Now that we have established my reason for being here, you can give me your phone number. I believe you owe me a date."

"What are you talking about? What date?"

"This is our third random meeting."

"Okay. And." Maxine folded her arms across her chest. "What if I'm not ready to give you my phone number?"

"You agreed to go out with me if we met again randomly. Remember."

"Oh yeah, I did say that. I guess a deal is a deal." Maxine recited her phone number for Eli as he entered the information into his phone.

"Maxine, come on, the car's here," a woman with short auburn locs called out.

"I'm coming," Maxine yelled back in response.

Turning back to Eli, she gave him a subtle smile. "I have to go. I'm sure I'll hear from you soon."

"Go ahead. I need to get inside. My pastor is waiting for me. I'll be calling you, pretty lady. Be sure to answer."

"We'll see," Maxine said, joining her lunch companions.

Eli watched until Maxine was out of sight. "Lord, that woman is fine. Um, mm, mmm."

Pastor Scott was busy scanning the menu when the hostess escorted Eli to the table. "Hey Doc, what's going on, man? Take a seat. I know how you feel about carbonated drinks, so I ordered your usual ice water with lemon," he said, laying the menu down in front of Eli.

"I appreciate that, Pastor." Before taking a seat across from Pastor Scott, Eli extended his hand for a handshake. He picked up the menu resting on the table and scanned the offerings.

Kea, their server, approached the table carrying a tray of beverages. “Hey, guys, how's it going today?” she asked, placing a glass of ice water and a small bowl of sliced lemons in front of Eli. She then placed a glass filled with hot water and a Dr. Pepper in front of Pastor Scott.

“See, that's why we keep coming back here, Kea. You always take good care of us. Whenever we come, I insist on being seated in your section,” Pastor Scott quipped. He removed his utensils from the cloth napkin and placed them in the glass of hot water.

“You know I'm going to look out for my favorite guests. I want you to keep coming to see me.”

Pastor Scott was known for his large tips when he and Eli dined together. The gesture was simple for him since he never paid the tab for their meals.

After reciting their orders, Eli waited for Kea to step away, allowing them some privacy. He chose a thick sliced lemon wedge from the bowl on the table. Squeezing the juice into his glass of water, he dropped the remnant back in the bowl. He stirred the mixture with a straw before taking a sip.

Readjusting in his chair, Pastor Scott rested his arms on the table and folded his hands. “Elder Clayton, I appreciate your meeting me for lunch today. I know you're a busy man running the dealership, and I didn't give you much notice.”

“It's alright, Pastor. I don't mind,” Eli lied. There were rare occasions when Pastor Scott wanted to meet with him just because. Most of their meetings included a toothy grin from Pastor Scott, followed by an open hand. Eli often considered moving his membership and money to a different church, but as big as Chicago was, the church circle was small. He didn't want to go from one leech to another. Other than the constant request for financial backing, Eli didn't mind offering his full support to the church.

“Praise God. The ministry has had a steady rise in youth

membership. I always say a church full of youth is a living church. Young people draw other young people. Within a few years, they grow up and start their own families and bring them to the church, continuing the cycle of growth."

Kea returned with their meals. "Alright, guys. Pastor Scott, you had the eight-ounce filet and lobster tail." She placed the hot plate on the table in front of Pastor Scott. Turning to Eli, she continued, "Mr. Clayton, you had the Chilean sea bass." Kea sat the plate in front of Eli and took a step back. "Is there anything else I can get for you guys?"

"No, we're fine," Pastor Scott said, slicing a piece of steak. He quickly bowed his head, saying grace before opening his mouth and savoring the bite. Slicing off another piece, Pastor Scott waved the steak firmly attached to his fork, through the air. "Where was I," he said. "Oh, yeah." He shoved the steak in his mouth and spoke between bites. "With the rapid growth of the youth, I think it's time we added more things to keep them interested. You know what I mean?"

Eli nodded but chose not to comment. He was more interested in consuming his fish than hearing another one of Pastor Scott's grand ideas. Though he appeared to listen with serious intent, Eli wanted to interrupt his charade and ask how much money he was requesting this time.

Oblivious to Eli's irritation, Pastor Scott continued to munch and pitch his proposal. "See, Doc, what I want to do is purchase the land next to the church and build a family life center. The young people of this city are dying off like a modern-day genocide. The center will give them a safe place with age-appropriate activities. I want a gym for basketball and volleyball games, a few classrooms with computers where they can do homework, and a cafeteria where they can have a hot meal every day."

Pastor Scott gulped down his Dr. Pepper. "Elder Clayton,

we're in the heart of Englewood. They need our ministry. People need to know Pastor Lee and Christ the True Vine is not the only place of worship available to them. I mean, I respect the man and all that he has accomplished since taking over the church. Between you and me, I believe he's becoming too commercial. You know what I mean."

"Yes, sir, Pastor, I understand. I like your idea. The members of the community can surely benefit from a center such as the one you envision. What is your plan for fundraising? I assume you have a plan in place."

Balancing his knife and fork, Pastor Scott cut a piece of lobster tail and dipped it in warm butter sauce. "That's where you come in, Doc. I was thinking maybe we can raffle off a brand-new car or maybe even a small SUV. We can sell the tickets for twenty-five or fifty dollars."

Squeezing his chin, Eli tilted his head to the side. "I see. Tell me, Pastor, how do I play into this?" Eli figured since he owned the dealership, Pastor Scott would ask for some sort of discount.

"Elder, you have an entire lot full. Surely it won't be a problem for you to donate one to the church."

Eli lowered the glass he had just picked up, causing a slight thump. He tried to mask his discontent but failed. He cleared his throat and pressed his back against the chair. "Donate? You want me to donate a new vehicle? That's mighty big, Pastor. I need to pray about this one."

"What's there to pray about? It's not like you're hurting. Like I said, you have a lot full. One won't be missed."

"Can I get you guys anything else, perhaps some dessert?" Kea asked, looking from Pastor Scott to Eli. They were so caught up in their conversation they hadn't noticed her approach.

"No. It's about time for me to get back to work," Eli answered, thankful for the distraction.

Pastor Scott held up his hand. “This was plenty for me. We’ll take the check now, if you don’t mind.”

“Alright guys.” Kea placed the folder containing their bill on the edge of the table, being careful to place it at an equal distance between the two men.

Eli knew the drill. Pastor Scott always expected him to pay. This time would be different. Eli was prepared to let the bill stay on the table for as long as needed. He would never disrespect Pastor Scott by asking Kea to split the check. However, today he would not foot the bill.

Pastor Scott reached for the folder containing the check and scanned the contents. He raised his eyebrow at the total and reached for his wallet.

“I’ll take care of this, Doc,” Pastor Scott said, retrieving the wallet from his pocket.

“Thank you, Pastor. I appreciate it.” Eli sat in quiet amusement.

Obvious shock registered on Pastor Scott’s face. He was prepared to leave a generous tip but had no intention of paying the over $150.00 bill. Not that he couldn’t afford to pay the bill, he didn’t think he should have to. There was no way he would allow Eli to show him up.

Removing a credit card from his wallet, Pastor Scott placed it inside the folder. He added a $50.00 tip and signed the enclosed slip. Pushing the folder aside, he directed his attention back to Eli.

“I’ll get you some more information concerning the plans for the center, and we can go from there.”

“That’ll work.” Eli pushed back from the table and stood. He extended his hand for another handshake before walking away. He’d heard every word Pastor Scott spoke concerning the new project he wanted to start, but all Eli could think about was Maxine. Thoughts he had to admit were not at all holy.

Seven

Maxine tapped the screen to end a call and placed her cell phone on the table beside her. She felt indifferent, not allowing herself to be excited or preparing for disappointment. Instead, she would let things play out organically. As promised, Eli hadn't hesitated to call. At least he'd waited until the next day to call instead of reaching out the same day. She wrestled with her decision to entertain Eli's company. What if he was a freak or a gross eater?

Her mind drifted back to what she considered her worst dinner date ever. One of her co-workers had set her up on a blind date. Something she rarely did, but out of boredom, she figured, why not? The date was a disaster from start to finish. Maxine rolled her eyes, reflecting on the night.

She arrived at the restaurant on time, only to find the guy already seated with an empty beer mug and a half-eaten appetizer. She slid into the booth across from the unattractive man. He offered to share the remaining appetizer with her, to which she refused.

The guy made it a point to let her know he was using a gift

card. A fact that wouldn't have mattered, except he made sure she didn't order anything that would exceed his gift card balance. He'd even suggested menu items that fell into the range of what he wanted to spend on her meal. His meal, however, was one of the more expensive items on the menu.

Counting the minutes until she could part his company, Maxine averted her attention elsewhere while pretending to be interested in what he had to say. She inserted appropriate responses so he would be none the wiser about her lack of attention. After a grueling hour and a half of watching him eat with his mouth open and dropping food and sauce all over his stretched out t-shirt, she was disgusted. The final straw came when he begged the manager for a discount because of the restaurant being out of various food items. The look on Maxine's face revealed her discomfort. The manager looked at Maxine with pity and agreed to take five dollars off the bill. Maxine's date acted as though he'd won a prize.

That was it. Maxine refused to endure the date any longer. Excusing herself, she grabbed her purse and left, only to find him hot on her heels. He insisted on walking her to her car. To make matters worse, the guy attempted to pull her in for a kiss when she offered him a polite handshake. She was mortified. Forcing her way out of his embrace, she jumped in her car and sped off, vowing to never go on another blind date.

The thought of a repeat experience gave her pause. What if her date with Eli was like the blind date? First lady or not, she knew she would not go through with it.

Maxine picked up her phone and located Eli's number. She needed to end this before it got started. Looking at the phone number on her screen, she reconsidered, surmising it wouldn't be fair to judge Eli based on an experience she had with another man. At least she had seen Eli multiple times. Unlike the blind date. She couldn't vouch for Eli's table manners, but she would give him the benefit of the doubt. Maxine decided she wouldn't form premature opinions of him, but she also wouldn't take anything that seemed off about him for granted. Saturday night would be here before she knew it. Until then, she would reserve her opinions.

Eli stood in front of the bathroom mirror and filled his hand with foam shaving cream. He smoothed the white fluff over his head, cheeks, and neck, then rinsed the remnants from his hands. Using a straight razor, he glided the sharp blade over his skin. Satisfied with his shave, he left the bathroom and entered his massive closet, contemplating the outfit for his date with Maxine.

Thinking of Maxine, Eli displayed a wide grin. He hadn't hesitated to call her after receiving her phone number. He would have called right after leaving the restaurant but chose to wait. Being too eager could make him look desperate. When she suggested another chance meeting be the determining factor of her going on a date with him, Eli prayed he would see her again. She was a beautiful, classy woman whom he wanted to know better.

With the positions he held, both in ministry and business, it wasn't uncommon for women to approach him. Some attractive, some not. He often had to weed out the women who had ill intentions from those with genuine interest. Eli was yet to determine Maxine's intentions, but he didn't quite care. She intrigued him. He was willing to see what the future held with her.

Glancing at his watch, he realized he'd better get going. Maxine had given him the address to a condo downtown, which would give them plenty of time to make their 8:00 dinner reservation.

Eli arrived at the address, parked his vehicle, and headed inside. A portly gentleman wearing a black suit, whom Eli figured was building security, sat behind a glass desk. The man stood as Eli approached.

"Good evening, sir. How may I be of assistance?"

"I'm here to see Ms. Miller in 1801," Eli stated.

"Your name is?" the man asked, scanning a slip of paper laying on the desk.

"Eli Clayton."

"Ah hah," the man replied, tapping on Eli's name. He handed Eli a slip of paper. "The elevators are to your right. When you press her floor, you will need to enter the code listed here." He pointed to a three-digit code on the paper. "This is a single use code." The man stated in a flat tone. "Turn right off the elevator to find Miss Miller's unit."

"Thank you."

Eli took the paper from the man and strode toward the elevator. He nodded as he looked around. Maxine's building appeared to be secure. Although it was located downtown, this was Chicago, a place known for crime. He felt the added security was ideal, especially for a single woman.

Stepping into the elevator, Eli followed the instructions given to him by the attendant. He was a bit surprised Maxine had asked him to come to her condo, rather than meeting him in the lobby. He decided not to make a big deal out of it. They were both adults, after all.

The ride up was fast. The elevator doors opened, and he stepped into a long hallway. He turned right and looked for Maxine's unit. Cupping his hand over his mouth, Eli did a quick check of his breath.

~

The chime of the doorbell flowed throughout the condo, prompting a wide grin to spread across Maxine's lips, rivaling a Cheshire cat. She stood in the full-length mirror, assessing her appearance. There was no doubt in her mind, she looked good. She had taken careful steps all day, preparing for her evening with Eli.

Maxine waited a few additional moments before approaching the door. She didn't want to appear anxious at his arrival. Pressing her hands against the door, she looked through the peephole to gain a sneak peek at her guest.

Maxine snatched the door open, startling Eli. "You have got to be kidding me." Her booming voice bounced off the walls.

Eli looked around in confusion. There was no way this woman was addressing him with such a demeaning tone. Realizing no one was standing behind him, he took a step back. "I beg your pardon."

"I spent all day getting ready for this date, and you had the nerve to come over here in jeans. Are you kidding me?"

Eli assessed his appearance. He felt his denim Tom Ford jeans, white pinstripe button-down shirt, and black sport coat were more than appropriate for dinner at The Signature Room. "You're joking, right? Although you look beautiful, I don't have a problem postponing this evening's plans for another time."

Eli was looking forward to his evening with Maxine, but he had no problem walking away, even though he'd almost drooled at the sight of her in the skin-tight metallic gold thigh length dress. The deep V-neck that stopped midway between her cleavage and waist left little to his imagination. As much as he liked her, Eli would not allow Maxine to disrespect him.

Relenting, Maxine pasted on a smile. "I'm only kidding. Give me a moment to grab my handbag and I'll be ready." She turned away and rolled her eyes. She hadn't been kidding. Maxine was prepared to slam the door in his face until she spied the Berluti shoes he was wearing. Being a lover of high end fashion, she inspected his outfit further, acknowledging the quality. The loafers alone carried a price tag of over two grand. Maxine shook off thoughts of the horrible blind date, forcing herself to remain in the moment. She wouldn't write Eli off now, but if their date was less than stellar, she would not subject herself to a second date.

MAXINE CURLED HER LIPS INTO A HALF SMILE WHEN ELI opened the passenger door to his black Bentley Bentayga S. The newmarket tan interior with black quilted stitching was breathtaking. Maxine slid inside and fastened her seatbelt. They rode the short distance to the John Hancock Center in silence.

Eli stole glances at Maxine as he drove. Tinted windows allowed him to admire her curves undetected. He arrived at 875 North Michigan Avenue, parked his vehicle, and hurried around to the passenger side to let Maxine out. He extended his elbow to escort her inside.

"Thank you, but I'm fine," she said, tapping him on the elbow.

Continuing inside, they made their way to the ninety-fifth floor. "Mr. Clayton how are you?" the maître'd greeted as the couple approached. We have a table ready for you by the window. Right this way."

"He said your name like he knows you," Maxine quipped as they trailed behind the maître'd.

"He should. I dine here at least once a month."

"I see."

Maxine scanned the room. She raised her eyebrow in delight as she admired the restaurant's layout and décor. She had to admit, if only to herself, Eli made an excellent choice for their first date. They arrived at the table and Maxine smiled at Eli's insistence on pulling her chair out.

She sat and took in the breathtaking view of the city. This was the treatment Maxine knew she deserved. Simple things she felt she could never have with Jonathan as long as he remained married. Maxine dreaded not being able to go to restaurants and theaters with Jonathan in the city, except for the instances when they portrayed it as being work related.

Early in their relationship, Jonathan had been willing to take a risk to please Maxine. They went on luxurious trips out of state and dined at restaurants that were known for discretion and protecting their patron's privacy. That all ended once his wife found evidence of his cheating. The threat of losing his family and the bulk of his wealth prompted Jonathan to continue his relationship with Maxine primarily behind the doors of her condo. At first, Maxine was fine with being a kept woman, but staying hidden was getting old.

As if she had summoned him, her phone buzzed, showing a text message from Jonathan.

Jonathan: Where are you???

She pasted on a tight-lipped smile. "Excuse me a moment, Eli. I need to reply to this message."

Maxine: I'm at my mother's house. She needed me to go over some insurance paperwork for her.

Jonathan: I'm growing tired of these excuses. Once again, I came by your place, and you are out gallivanting around.

Maxine: I know baby, I'm so sorry. I thought you would be home since it's Saturday night, so I thought this would be a good time for me to swing by mother's.

She waited a moment to see his reply. When he didn't respond, she placed her phone inside her handbag and returned her attention to Eli. He appeared to be scanning the menu.

"Sorry for the interruption. That was my mother."

Lowering the menu, Eli replied, "There's no need to apologize. Mothers are important. Is everything okay?"

"Yes, she's fine. She had a question about some insurance paperwork." Maxine picked up the menu and scanned the offerings. She smirked knowing she'd told the same lie to both men without flinching. "Everything looks appetizing. I guess I'll get the seafood pasta."

"The pasta is good here. I believe you'll enjoy it. I'm going to get the rack of lamb."

Maxine slid a manicured fingernail over the offerings on the menu. Content with her selection, she closed the menu and looked out the window, observing the city's skyline. She took a deep breath and directed her attention back to Eli. "This place is amazing. The view is breathtaking."

"I'm glad you like it." Eli folded his hands and placed them on the table. "The view does not compare to how stunning you are this evening. There is nothing inside nor outside that compares to your beauty."

"Thank you, Eli. You know what to say to score some points, don't you?"

"I only speak what I believe to be true."

"Hold that thought," Maxine interrupted. She opened the menu once again and directed her attention to the server that had approached.

"I'm in the mood for a cocktail," she said, peering at Eli. She paused a beat, waiting to see if he would object to her ordering alcohol. When he didn't, she smiled and continued, "I'd like a glass of signature room punch, and for my meal, I'll have the seafood pasta."

"Excellent choice. Our seafood pasta includes crab, scallops, and shrimp. Is that okay with you?"

"That's fine," Maxine answered.

The server recorded Maxine's order and directed her attention to Eli. "And for you, sir?"

Eli replied without a second glance at the menu. "Give me the rack of lamb. I also want sautéed asparagus and roasted herb mushrooms. I'll take water with lemon to drink. You can bring it out with my meal."

"Yes, sir." The server gathered the menus from the table. "I'll get those orders put in right away." She turned to Maxine and continued, "I'll be back with your cocktail."

Staring at Maxine, Eli smiled, lifting only his right cheek.

"Why are you looking at me like that?" Maxine asked, keeping her tone neutral.

"I was just thinking how grateful I am to God for that third interaction we had."

Maxine tilted her head to the side, exposing a sparkling chain link diamond earring. "The third interaction?" she asked with a raised eyebrow.

Chuckling, Eli replied, "Don't get me wrong, sweetheart. I have enjoyed each of our interactions, but the third one got you here with me tonight. I guess it's all about timing. God is funny that way. I had never seen you before in my life. Then, we met three times in less than two months. It's like God dropped you from heaven just for me."

Maxine burst into laughter. "You started out good, but that last part was straight corny." She placed her hand on her chest and continued to laugh. "I've heard plenty pickup lines, as I'm sure you can imagine. I guess this is flirting church style. You are too much, Eli. Thank you. I needed that laugh."

Eli gazed at Maxine with a sheepish grin.

"Why are you looking at me like that?" Maxine asked, cutting off her laughter.

"No reason. It's nice to know I put a smile on your face. Personally, I could've been offended by your laughter, but I'm not. I like the sound of your laugh. It's cute. They say laughter is good for the soul."

"Um hmm," she replied.

The server returned and placed Maxine's cocktail on the table. "Your meals will be out soon."

Taking a sip, Maxine nodded. "This is delicious." She stirred the fruit around in her drink. "So, Eli, tell me about yourself. I know you're a minister. Do you have your own church?"

"No, I'm not a pastor. I'm an associate minister."

"What do you do for work?"

"I work in the auto industry. What about you, Maxine? What kind of work do you do? The last time I saw you, you and the ladies seemed to be dressed in business attire."

"My, aren't you observant," Maxine teased. "Since you were vague in your response, I'll do the same. I work in law."

"Yeah, I can see that." Eli replied with a nod.

"What's that supposed to mean?" Maxine sat up straight and crossed her arms.

"You seem to be a very calculated woman. Not impulsive. Based on our past interactions, you don't appear to be the type of woman to do stuff at random. You're more of a planner. Even if you don't tell anyone else until after your plan is in place. That's how lawyers are. I for one, wouldn't want an impulsive attorney. So yeah, the law field suits you."

"I guess we are different in that way. Judging by your actions when I first encountered you, followed by every other time we met, you make decisions on the fly. You said you don't like to delay the obvious, and it shows."

Eli leaned in. "Ah, you recall our conversation at the church. I like that. It shows you pay attention. I need a woman like you in my life."

Maxine placed her hand on her neck and purred. "Hmmm. Is that right?"

Nine

"Can I do this?" Maxine said aloud as she stood in the bathroom mirror removing her makeup. Dinner with Eli had gone better than she expected. What she thought would be an evening of forcing herself to make it through boring conversation littered with church talk turned out to be quite the opposite. Before their date, Maxine had made up in her mind Eli would be nothing more than a means to an end. Instead, what she found was a man that treated her with respect. Their conversation had been easy. He made her laugh. As much as she tried to remain guarded, Eli broke through her walls of defense as if they were made of cotton candy.

Being with Jonathan, Maxine had forgotten what it was like being a man's number one. The men in her past never looked at her the way Eli did. He didn't look at her with lust. She felt as though he was seeing right through her. Reading her like a book.

The phone rang, rescuing Maxine from her thoughts.

"I couldn't wait any longer," Rashida yelled into the phone before Maxine even said hello.

"Dang. Why are you yelling? You realize there is an ear on this end of the phone, don't you?"

"My bad, girl. I had to know how your date with Sherman went."

"Sherman?" Maxine shook her head, wondering if she'd heard her friend correctly.

"Yeah, you know, like the Nutty Professor. Sherman, Sherman, Sherman." Rashida clapped her hands as she repeated the name.

"Don't call him Sherman. That's not cool, Rashida."

"Hold up. Did you just call my whole name? I must have struck a nerve. You're defending him? What did I miss?"

"You didn't miss anything. He's a nice guy."

"Wow. I don't know what to say. You caught me by surprise. I just knew you were about to have me cracking up about how bad the date was. Where did he take you? Come on, Maxine, give me something."

"For starters, he picked me up in a Bentley."

"Nice," Rashida replied, stretching out the word.

"I know, right. At first, it pissed me off when I saw he was wearing jeans, but after I saw his vehicle I was like okay, let's see where this goes. He took me to The Signature Room."

"I love that restaurant," Rashida squealed. "The food is delicious, and the view is amazing."

"You've been there?"

"Several times. I told you, I gets mine." Realizing Maxine had grown silent, Rashida redirected the conversation. "Wait a minute. You've never been to The Signature Room? How is that? You live downtown and I know Jonathan got enough bank to afford it."

"No, I hadn't been there before tonight. It's not like Jonathan and I can go frolicking all over the city. He's married and well known. Pretty much any place downtown we go, someone will recognize him."

"See, that's the very reason why I don't fool with married men. I know the men I deal with date more than just me. We have that understanding, but none of the men I deal with have wives."

Maxine became indignant. She didn't need Rashida highlighting the fact Jonathan was married. "Look, you want me to finish telling you about this date or what?"

"I'm just trippin, girl. Go ahead."

"You know what? There isn't much more to tell. We had a great conversation, and he made me laugh. After dinner, he dropped me off. End of story."

"Did he try to kiss you?"

"No. He was a perfect gentleman the whole time. I caught him checking me out throughout the night. This date wasn't at all what I expected."

"Dude is so unattractive. I don't see how you can do it."

"I thought the same thing, not only when the date started but also after I got home. In fact, I was thinking about that very thing when you called. The date went well enough that I'm considering it, which is a good thing. The cosmetic things like his weight and jacked up skin are fixable. If he had those issues and was a jerk, this would be a simple decision. I don't care how bad I want to be a first lady. I would wait until a better option comes along, but tonight there was something there. At least enough for me to continue to explore this."

"See, that's the part I'm concerned about. If you pursue this, what's going to happen to you and Jonathan?"

"Please. You don't need to be concerned. I would be a fool if I allowed my life to revolve around Jonathan's actions. The same way God made one man, He made more. I have never put all my trust in a man. I always have a backup plan. If I decide to move forward with Eli, I will do it knowing I'll have to let Jonathan go."

"You're better than me, because there ain't no way I would let go of a sure thing for a maybe."

"You would if it was worth it. Especially with the way Jonathan has treated me lately, making a change just may be exactly what I need.

Maxine and Rashida continued to talk about the evening and their weekend plans until Rashida received another call. Maxine prepared for bed and slid under Egyptian cotton sheets. She snuggled, adjusting her pillow just right. Tonight was different. For the first time in a long time, she wished she wasn't alone.

Ten

The phone felt like a weight in Eli's hand. It had been several days since his date with Maxine, he still hadn't heard from her. He realized the date started off strained. At times he felt like Maxine was testing him, but he was confident he hadn't taken the bait. He was taken aback by her reaction to his choice of wearing jeans on their date to the point he almost walked away, but there was something about her that kept him intrigued. By the way she looked at him, he knew her choice of beverage was another clear sign of her testing him. A test he passed with ease.

Maxine put up a good front, but Eli was more interested in getting to know the woman behind the façade. Thoughts of Maxine continued to flood his mind. He couldn't wait any longer. He unlocked his phone and opened his messaging app. He clicked on the text thread of his and Maxine's previous messages and dropped his head.

"I'm such an idiot. I never hit send on the last message. No wonder I haven't heard from her." Eli read over the text and figured although late, it still applied. He pressed the send button and hoped for a reply.

Eli: Hello Beautiful, how's it going? I was thinking about you and wanted to reach out. I had a great time at dinner.

Several minutes passed before Eli looked down at his phone. Wrinkles spread across his forehead as anticipation and disappointment competed for dominance in his mind. Perhaps he'd waited too long. There was a possibility he'd misinterpreted the evening. Maybe Maxine didn't enjoy the evening as much as he had. Who was he fooling? There's no way a woman as beautiful as Maxine would have a genuine interest in him. Time was passing quickly.

Eli re-read the message he sent to Maxine. He wondered if wording the message another way would have prompted a response. Resigned, he returned his attention to his work computer. Without fail, he could always count on the dealership to provide a distraction. The chime of the phone startled Eli, causing him to knock the device to the floor. A heavy grunt escaped him as he bent over to retrieve the phone.

Pastor Scott: Hey Doc. How's your schedule? I want to follow up with you on the vehicle raffle. Are you free for lunch today?

This was not the message Eli wanted to receive. He wasn't interested in buying lunch for his pastor, and donating a vehicle was out of the question. Eli didn't want to cause friction with his pastor, but he also didn't want to be viewed as a money tree. Yes, his father had blessed him with a nice nest egg, and his business was very successful, but experience told him if he continued to give every time the pastor asked, the request would never cease.

Eli: I'm tied up today. As for the vehicle, I can provide a compact car at wholesale. I'll also absorb the cost of tax, tags, and title registration.

Eli pressed send on the message and prepared himself for the counteroffer from his pastor. As expected, the phone chimed with the message notification tone. Eli took a deep breath, mentally preparing himself for his pastor's rebuttal. He lifted the phone and read the incoming message.

Maxine: Hi Eli. Sorry for the delay. I was in a meeting. I'm good, and you? I had a good time the other night as well.

Eli's smile widened. He didn't hesitate to text back.

Eli: I'm good. Hope you'll give me the opportunity to see you again, perhaps this weekend.

Maxine: I'm sure that can be arranged. What do you have in mind?

Eli: I want to have some fun. How's your bowling game?

Maxine: Ew. Putting my feet in rented shoes and throwing a heavy ball is not my idea of fun.

Eli: How about a movie?

Maxine: Okay. Call me later. We can iron out the details. I need to get back to work.

Eli: Will do.

Eli laid the phone back on his desk. If Pastor Scott replied, it would have to wait. Eli refused to let anything ruin his mood. He had a date to plan.

Eleven

MAXINE STEPPED ASIDE AND WAITED FOR ELI TO OPEN her car door. She tapped her foot and waited for him to get in. Jerking the seatbelt, she pressed her back into the seat. Maxine struggled to check her attitude, but being with Eli right now was not what she wanted. Not after the night she'd spent with Jonathan. It was rare for Jonathan to sleep over, especially during the weekend. His wife's trip out of town gave him the freedom to stay overnight with Maxine. She savored every moment. Jonathan had satisfied the companionship and intimacy she craved. Reflecting on her time with Jonathan, her lips turned up into a warm smile just as Eli entered the vehicle.

Eli turned to Maxine and matched the smile he thought was for him. "As usual, you are so beautiful tonight." Even in a plain V-neck t-shirt, she looked like a model. He scanned her body, allowing his eyes to rest on her thighs. The jeans she wore fit like a glove. Her crossed legs allowed him to see the bright red sole of her shoes.

"I hope you're ready for a fun evening."

"Where are we going?" Maxine asked as Eli pulled away from

the curb.

"I thought we'd go to the dine-in movie theater on Michigan Avenue."

No longer able to hide her annoyance, Maxine folded her arms across her chest and let out an exasperated sigh. "I realize I live in the heart of downtown and there are plenty of places we could go, but you don't have to keep taking me to places pretty much around the corner from my home. I'm not restricted to a small perimeter."

She was regretting not cancelling this date with Eli. Maxine had every intention of doing so, but when Jonathan told her he had to leave shortly after she'd prepared brunch for them, she chose to keep the plans she'd made with Eli.

"We're not limited to downtown. I have no problem taking you anywhere your heart desires. We talked about a movie and I know the theater on Michigan Avenue is nice, but we can go somewhere else."

"Yeah, let's do that. I live here and there are plenty of options, but I get tired of downtown sometimes."

"How far are you willing to go?" Eli asked with a smirk.

Maxine furrowed her eyebrows. "What do you mean?" All decorum was out the window. She was straight Southside Chicago.

Eli laughed. "Calm down, beautiful. I mean, how far away are you willing to travel? I know of a great drive-in theater we can go to if you're up for the ride."

"Man, I thought I was about to have to get you together." Laughter erupted from Maxine. "As for the drive-in, that sounds fun. I haven't been to one since I was a kid."

Eli merged onto the Stevenson Expressway and set the cruise control. Vehicles zipped by, but he didn't seem to mind. He enjoyed having Maxine by his side. He felt the drive was an excellent opportunity for him and Maxine to get to know each other better. He pressed the volume button on the steering wheel, lowering the music playing throughout the vehicle.

Keeping the conversation casual, he asked, "How was work this week?"

"This was a long week. I was so ready to get out of there yesterday I didn't know what to do. They tried to work my poor little fingers to the bone. I'll be so glad when I no longer have to go to Freeman, Reynolds, and Associates. The partners are not the issue. It's the office staff that gets on my nerves most of the time. Who knows, maybe one day I'll get to live my dream of mentoring women and teenage girls. I believe every woman can be beautiful when she sees beauty within. I want to show them how to get there."

Pondering her statement, Eli thought of how he could help make her dream a reality. For now, he felt it best to live in the moment instead of focusing on a potential future. "This may sound a bit cliché, but I have to ask. How are you still single? You're a gorgeous woman. You have an illustrious career. Your place is amazing. From where I stand, you seem to have it all together. How has a man not wifed you yet?"

"How do you know I'm not single by choice? Not every woman wants to be somebody's wife."

"You're right. I guess I just assumed..."

"You know what they say about assuming," Maxine interrupted.

Eli relented. "I'm sorry, beautiful. I wasn't trying to offend you. From the moment I met you, I felt there was something special about you. Any man would be blessed to have you. I enjoy spending time with you and I'm honored to have the opportunity."

Maxine softened. She realized she was being hard on Eli without a cause. Even if she wasn't honest with him, Maxine knew she couldn't lie to herself. She wanted to be a wife. She wanted a man she could call her own. Jonathan took good care of her financial needs. He wasn't slack with her physical needs when he was available, but she wanted more.

She turned to Eli and answered honestly. "I'm single because I want a man that will not only love me, but he has to take care of me in every way. I refuse to have a man that can't support me as well as I'm able to support myself. I don't want a man just for the sake of having somebody."

Eli pulled into the drive-in and paid the admission. He drove around to the area for the movie *The Five Heartbeats.*

"I love this movie," Maxine exclaimed. "I don't care how much time has passed. This movie never gets old."

"I agree. That's why I like this place, they tend to play older movies. These new movies can't touch the old school."

The two reclined their seats and settled in for the movie. Eli tuned his radio to the station given by the ticket agent. He pulled up the website for concessions on his phone and ordered refreshments for them.

"This place is nice," Maxine acknowledged. "I especially like not having to leave the vehicle for refreshments."

"Yeah, it's a nice option, although you wouldn't have to go get the refreshments, anyway. When you're with me, you wouldn't have to worry yourself with anything like that, period. As much as it's in my power to do, I'll get you what you need."

"Be careful. You talk a good game. I'm the woman that will challenge those words with no other reason than to see if you are lying."

"I'm a man of my word. If I say it, I'm going to make sure it's done. My dad always told me a man is only as good as his word. If you can't keep your word, you're not benefiting anyone."

Rather than respond, Maxine made a mental note to test his statement. If he was the man he claimed to be, she just might be able to turn this toad into a prince.

Twelve

Eli gazed at Maxine as they rode in virtual silence back to her condo. He wondered what had her so deep in thought. It was obvious she was awake. Apart from a few hummed responses when he spoke, she hadn't spoken. One thing he didn't have to wonder was if she'd enjoyed the movie. They both had. It was obvious by the way they laughed, sang along, and danced to the music. Maxine perked up when the scene with Duck and his little sister hit the screen. She was all over the front seat, waving her arms and singing. Eli smiled at the recollection.

Everything seemed to change for Maxine during the church scene. Eli noticed Maxine had quieted down, but it wasn't until she dabbed at her eyes with her napkin that he realize she was in tears. He had watched *The Five Heartbeats* countless times. The church scene was touching, but it seemed to be something more for Maxine.

From the moment he laid eyes on her, she showed strength and confidence. He didn't believe she had a weak bone in her body. The dress she wore on their first date with the plunging neckline, despite knowing he was a minister, told him she was rebellious and cautioned him to stay away. Tonight, seeing her so vulnerable, so fragile, he knew his attraction to her wasn't just physical. Maxine Miller was the woman God had for him, and he was going to do everything in his power to make her his.

The vehicle eased to a stop as Eli pulled up in front of Maxine's building. "I had a great time with you this evening."

"I did too," Maxine admitted. "It's been years since I've been to a drive-in. I'm glad we went."

"Are you sure you won't reconsider grabbing a bite to eat? There are countless restaurants that we can hit up. The night is still young." Eli pointed at the illuminated clock on the dash.

"Thank you for the offer, but the snacks at the drive-in filled me up. I can't ingest another bite without making myself sick. Come to think of it, I haven't had that much junk food in God knows when. But I enjoyed every greasy and gooey bit of it."

Surrendering, Eli countered, "If you have time in your schedule, perhaps we can have lunch or something next week."

"I don't see why not. Let me check my schedule and I'll let you know." Maxine pressed the button to release her seatbelt.

"I'd be glad to walk you up," Eli said, turning off the ignition.

"That won't be necessary. I'm good." Maxine reached for the door handle.

"Wait a second. I can't believe I almost forgot." Eli opened the center console, pulled out a small bag, and handed it to Maxine.

"What's this?" Maxine asked, outlining the letters on the blue bag with her fingernail.

"I was out doing some shopping earlier. I saw this and thought it looked like you. Open it."

Maxine opened the bag and pulled out a small box. Giving Eli a sidelong glance, she opened the box and found a pair of three inch long gold mesh earrings. She pulled down the sun visor and opened the lighted mirror. Holding the earring box up to her ears, she spread her lips into a wide smile. "Eli, these are beautiful.

Thank you so much." She leaned over and wrapped her arms around him, placing a kiss on his cheek.

"You're welcome, beautiful. I'm glad you like them." He took a deep breath and placed a firm grip on the steering wheel. Resisting the urge to return Maxine's embrace was not an easy feat.

Thirteen

"Why didn't you tell me you and Jonathan broke up?"

Sitting up in the bed, Maxine pulled the phone away from her ear and squeezed her eyes shut. The screech in Rashida's voice was deafening. "What are you talking about?" She yawned into the phone and rubbed her forehead.

"I know you went out with that Eli guy a few times, but I didn't know it progressed to the point of you dumping Jonathan."

"Girl, slow down. It's too early in the morning for this nonsense. What makes you think I broke up with Jonathan?"

Rashida exhaled, forcing the air out loud enough for Maxine to hear her frustration. "Well, when I texted you last week, you said you were at the movies with Eli. Later that same night, I saw Jonathan at Hot Glue all hugged up on some young stripper looking chick. It wasn't even two hours later."

"Hold up. What in the world is Hot Glue?"

"It's a nightclub on the North side. I thought I told you

about it before." Rashida snapped her fingers. "I know I did because I asked you to go with me a couple years ago. You turned up your bougie little nose as soon as I said the name of the club."

"Oh yeah, I remember when you asked me to go to that little ratchet club. I can't believe you thought I would even consider going there."

"You see how your mind works? You're so bougie. Out of everything I said to you, the thing you focused on was the nightclub. Yoo-hoo earth to Maxine. Did you not hear me say your man was in the club with another woman? I know it wasn't his wife. Girlfriend looked like she was young enough to be his daughter. You're going around spending time with an Oompa Loompa while Jonathan is trading your butt in for a newer model."

"Trick, I know you didn't." Maxine was furious. Rashida had her nerve. Maxine knew she could pull any man she wanted.

"I got your trick, Maxine. Don't get it twisted, I'm just trying to help you out. What you're not about to do is start calling me out of my name."

"What bug do you have up your butt, Rashi? Let's not forget you started this by trying to call me old. It's way too early in the morning for this drama. Thank you for your concern, but I'm good. I'll talk to you later."

Maxine ended the call, denying Rashida the opportunity for rebuttal. Pillows fell to the floor as Maxine shoved the bed covers away from her. Her phone chimed. She picked it up and rolled her eyes before reading the incoming text.

> Rashida: I was going to invite you out tonight since I know you and Jonathan don't do stuff on the weekend, but since you want to be petty and hang up, I'll give you some space. Call me when you get over your attitude.

Rolling her eyes, Maxine tossed the phone onto her bed. If what Rashida said was true, it would force her to end things with Jonathan sooner than she planned. It was one thing to be Jonathan's mistress with no hope of becoming his wife. To be one of God only knows how many of Jonathan's side chicks was insane. There was no way she was going to put up with that.

Being Saturday, Maxine was sure she wouldn't see Jonathan. He claimed it was time he spent with his family. Now she knew better. Curling her lips into a mischievous grin, she scooped up her phone and scrolled through her contacts. Her days with Jonathan were sure to be numbered. It was time for her to escalate her plan to secure her future. She thought of sending a text but reconsidered. The shock value was part of the fun.

The aroma of freshly ground coffee beans filled the bottom floor of Eli's house, tantalizing his senses. He pulled his favorite mug from the cabinet and filled it with the hot liquid. The phone rang just as he lifted the mug to his lips. His eyes widened when he saw Maxine's name on the display.

"Well, well, well, to whom, or shall I say what, do I owe this pleasure?" He tried to sound dapper, but inside he was celebrating.

"You make it seem like I never call you," Maxine replied with a purr.

"Sweetheart, that's because you don't. Please don't misunderstand. I'm not complaining. It's nice hearing your voice early in the morning."

"Ah, okay. I was about to say, if it's an issue, I can hang up."

"Nah, that's unnecessary. What's going on?" Eli took a sip from his coffee and settled in for what he hoped would be a lengthy conversation.

"When we returned from the drive-in you mentioned getting together for lunch or something. I realize you reached out a few times with no response, but last week was not good for me. Work was overwhelming and I'm dealing with some other personal stuff. I didn't respond to your calls or messages because I didn't want to burden you with the drama."

"You could never burden me, Maxine. I'm a big guy. I can handle a lot," Eli jested. "What do you have going on today? Maybe I can take you to breakfast or lunch. Perhaps we could go for a walk or something. It's your call."

Maxine paused as if she was considering Eli's suggestion. "I'm not sure where you live, so it may be too late for breakfast, but brunch would be nice. What do you think?"

A loud screech echoed throughout the room as Eli stood and pushed his chair back. "Brunch is good. Give me a little while and I'll be by to pick you up. Is there anywhere in particular you'd like to go?"

"I was thinking," Maxine hummed, "I'll cook for you. What do you think?"

Eli's eyebrows shot up in surprise. "You're inviting me over to your place? Are you sure?"

"Of course, I'm sure, Eli. It's not like you're a stranger." Maxine released an exasperated sigh. "Don't worry, I know how to behave myself. You'll still be a minister after you leave. I won't soil your reputation."

"I'm not worried about that at all, sweetheart. I, alone, am responsible for my actions. It's just, your offer surprised me, that's all. This is the first time you've invited me over."

"Do you want to come over or not, Eli? I'm getting dizzy from all these circles you're running around in." Maxine's frustration was clear in her tone.

Not willing to frustrate her any further, Eli agreed to brunch at her home. He dressed without hesitation, splashed on his favorite cologne, and made his way to Maxine's. He didn't want to appear too eager, but playing it cool was becoming a challenge. He'd began to doubt things with her would go anywhere after she ignored multiple calls and texts from him. Her call reaffirmed his belief that Maxine Miller was the woman God destined for him.

Fourteen

"I don't know what's on the menu, but something smells delicious." Eli stepped inside Maxine's condo and greeted her with a hug.

"It didn't take you long to get here. Come to think of it, you've never told me where you live." Maxine acknowledged.

"I have a house in Burr Ridge. Traffic was light, so it was a short drive."

Maxine took Eli by the hand and led him to the kitchen. She motioned him towards a bistro style table and chairs. "Have a seat and I'll get the food." Maxine brought two crystal flutes filled with chilled pineapple juice and two bowls of cut fruit.

"Would you like some help with the food?" Eli asked, pushing his chair back.

"No, I got it." She stepped into the kitchen and returned with two full plates. She placed one in front of Eli and sat down, sitting the other plate on the table.

"Did you cook all this yourself?" Eli took a deep breath, inhaling the aroma of the maple bacon waffles and crispy fried chicken strips. He speared a piece of cantaloupe from the bowl of fruit.

“Yes. Don’t let the beauty fool you, I have skills. I can throw down in the kitchen. My grandmother taught me how to cook.” Maxine waved her fork in the air. “My future husband is in for a treat.”

“I would say so. These waffles are the best I’ve had.”

“I’m glad you’re enjoying them.”

“How long have you lived here?” Eli inquired. He observed the open space. “That view is outstanding.” He peered out of the glass picture window and door that led to the balcony.

“Thank you, Eli.” Maxine paused for a sip of juice before continuing. “I’ve been here about a year and a half. I love the view as well. In fact, that was one of the biggest selling points for me. I love to sit out on the balcony and observe the city. There’s always something going on. You should see the lakefront during Harbor Fest when all the boats gather on the water. It’s a sight to see.”

“I can imagine it is a sight from this angle. I haven’t seen it like that, however I have taken part.”

“Is that right?” Maxine raised up on her elbows, drawing closer to Eli. “You’ve participated in Harbor Fest? How?”

“I took my boat out. My parents enjoy the water. Sometimes I take them, and other times I take my buddies.”

“Wait a minute. You have a boat? Let’s not just skirt past that fact. I bet your parents and buddies, as you call them, are not the only ones you take with you.” Maxine’s responses were spilling out like rapid fire. “You can’t tell me you don’t take women with you. What kind of boat is it?”

Eli noted the change in Maxine’s tone. He detected what he thought was a hint of jealousy when she mentioned women going on the boat with him. “I have a Cayman F920. Don’t worry, I can assure you I haven’t taken any women out on the boat other than my mother and my chef. If you're interested, I would love to take you one day."

"That sounds like fun." Maxine struggled to downplay her excitement. The more she was learning about Eli, the more satisfied she became with her decision to pursue him. If he was being honest with her about the Cayman, she knew he was holding back his true wealth. The boat he described was a yacht valued at over seven million dollars. He also mentioned he had a house in Burr Ridge, one of the richest communities in Illinois. Maxine was cool with the information Eli was sharing. However, it was the part he wasn't sharing that held her captive. She was determined to find out who Eli Clayton was, finances and all.

Following their meal, Maxine invited Eli to join her on the balcony. It was time for her to get to know him better. Their previous dates had been riddled with safe subjects. Hearing of Jonathan's side chick, she knew she needed to solidify her backup plan.

A gentle breeze kissed their cheeks, providing a slight reprieve from the warm sun.

"I can see why you like it here. The view was nice from inside, but this is beautiful. I imagine it's even better at night."

"Yes, the view at night is breathtaking." Maxine paused, staring at the water. She sighed before continuing. "Truth is, I'm growing tired of this place. I know I'm the only one living here, but this condo is just too small. The location is phenomenal, but I could do without the super high mortgage. Especially with the way things are going at work."

Eli turned to her. "You're having issues at work? What's going on? Perhaps I can help."

Maxine slumped in her chair, feigning frustration. "There are rumors the founding partner has gotten involved in some shady business dealings. The entire firm is being affected. It's only a matter of time before it all comes crashing down. When that happens, I don't know what I'm going to do. I can find another job, but this mortgage and my bills will not wait for me to figure it out." She spoke of the law firm for Eli's benefit, but in reality, Maxine was speaking about her relationship with Jonathan.

Holding her gaze, Eli brushed his thumb against Maxine's cheek. "Sweetheart, you don't have to worry about a thing. I know God is going to work everything out for you. You will be just fine. If you ask me, from what I can see, you will be even better than you are now."

"Is that so?" Maxine queried, leaning toward him.

"Yes, it's so. There's so much I wish I could tell you, but now is not the time."

Extending her arms, Maxine shook her head. "No one else is around." She pretended she was looking over the balcony. "I'm certain the people on the ground can't hear us either. You can tell me anything."

Folding her hands into his, Eli replied, "In time, my dear. All things will be revealed in time." Standing, he pulled Maxine up beside him. "It's a beautiful day. Let's go for a walk."

Maxine and Eli took to the street and padded around downtown Chicago. The more time she spent with him, the more she enjoyed his company. Not only did Eli make her laugh, but she also felt important to him. Their mutual love of travel kept them talking for hours. She relaxed in Eli's presence. She found she could be herself without the risk of judgement. Eli made it a point to tell her he would never judge her, and she believed him.

Fifteen

"Girl, I can't believe you have been dating Eli for four whole months. I'm gon' be honest, Maxine, I didn't think you could actually pull it off. He's so different from the men I'm used to seeing you with. You surprised me, for real."

"I know. Eli *is* different, but I like him." Maxine placed her phone between her ear and shoulder while she sifted through her handbag until she felt the cold metal of her keys. "The thing I like most about him is the way he treats me. The man treats me like I'm a straight up queen. No lie. The best part is it's not about sex, which is good, because I don't think I could handle that right now. He's a cool guy, but I still don't see him in a romantic way."

"How are you making it work with him and Jonathan? That seems like a lot of juggling. What were you thinking? I've dated two men at the same time before, but it was casual and they knew it. The difference with you is, you and Jonathan have been together for a while. Now, you seem to be getting serious about Eli. I find it hard to believe neither of them suspects you of seeing somebody else."

"Please. Rashida, I have both men wrapped around my finger.

Eli is straight up love struck. In his eyes, I can do no wrong. That's a good thing, because I plan to make him long term. I told you I'm going to be a first lady. Let's not forget that's the whole point of me spending time with Eli. As for Jonathan, he thinks I don't know about his little play toy you saw him with at the nightclub. Honestly, I don't even care anymore. As long as he keeps paying the bills and lining my pockets, I'm good." Maxine turned the key and opened the door to her condo.

"Is that so?" a male voice cut into her conversation, catching her off guard.

Maxine expelled a cough as the breath caught in her throat. "Jonathan, what... what are you doing here?" she stammered, closing the door with her foot.

"Baby, I'm just like Jesus. You never know when I'm coming. Don't stutter now. You were talking clear when you said I'm paying the bills and lining your pockets. Where have you been?" Jonathan spat as he rose from the couch. A small crack snaked through the glass table from the impact of his beer bottle being slammed down. "Who is Eli? Is he the reason you're never here when you're supposed to be?" Flower petals scattered as he snatched the card from a fresh bouquet and threw it at her.

"Wait a minute," Maxine shrieked. "You can't be coming up in here destroying my home. Who do you think you are?"

"I pay the bills in this place. I can do what I want, including destroying anything in here." He took the vase and slammed it against the wall.

"That's enough, Jonathan. I want you out of here. I don't care what bills you pay. My name is on this deed. You don't own anything in here, especially me. My grandma Frances taught me early in life. I'm a much right woman."

Angry words spewed from Jonathan like venom followed by alcohol induced spittle. "Much right woman, what kind of ignorant bull is that supposed to be?"

"It means I've got as much right to see Eli, or whoever else I want, as I have to see you. You have a wife, but I'm not her." Maxine pulled the door open. "Now I'm going to tell you for the last time. Get out of here and don't come back unless you're invited."

Jonathan slammed the door shut causing Maxine to stumble backwards. "You think this is some type of game, don't you? I let myself in and I will leave when I'm ready. Don't fool yourself into thinking you have power and authority that you don't."

"I don't know how much you have been drinking and I don't care. What I do know is if you don't leave on your own, I'll have you escorted out of here."

"I'd like to see you try it." Jonathan's words slurred.

"I'm not playing with you, Jonathan. Either leave now, or I'll call the police." Maxine looked around her living room in disgust. "Look at this place. All it will take the cops is one glance, and a whiff of your alcohol laced breath, and you'll be sobering up behind bars. I wonder what your precious wife would think about you then."

"I don't have time for this. I'm not worried about you, you raggedy—"

"Don't you dare," Maxine pressed, cutting him off mid-sentence. Once again, she opened the door. "Get out!"

Jonathan walked out the door and delivered a final warning. "I guarantee you'll be begging me to come back, but you can forget it. Women like you are a dime a dozen. You're going to regret whoring around on me."

Maxine pushed the door closed and rolled her eyes. A faint sound emanated from her phone. In the commotion, Maxine forgot she was on the phone with Rashida. She lifted the device to her ear. "Hello."

"Girl, are you okay? I thought I was gon' have to call the

police. When I heard all that noise in the background, I thought Jonathan was about to knock you out."

"Please, I'm fine. Jonathan knows better than to put his hands on me. I am not the one. Besides, he can't afford the negative publicity."

"Yeah, okay. Negative publicity or not, men will act a straight fool on a woman when he knows she's messing around with another man. If I were you, I would watch my back. There ain't no telling what he will do to you after this."

"I wish he would try something. I will blow his game all the way up." Maxine bent down to pick up the flowers. "Rashi, let me get off this phone so I can clean up this mess."

Maxine ended her call with Rashida and scanned her living room. She attempted to sound unbothered when she was talking to her friend, but it was only a front. Her heart was pounding. She didn't know what Jonathan would do in retaliation. During their relationship, Maxine had witnessed Jonathan perform many underhanded acts. So much of her life was tied to him. From her job to her home, he played a part in every area. The way she saw it, she had two options. Either smooth things over with Jonathan or speed up the process with Eli. Regardless of the choice, time was not on her side.

Sixteen

"Man, are you crazy?" Zachariah exclaimed, staring at his best friend and fellow minister. "I have known you for over ten years and you have done nothing this wild. What is it about this woman that made you lose your whole mind?"

Shaking his head, Eli placed the velvet box containing a four-carat diamond ring on the coffee table. "Dude, calm down. I know you think I'm crazy, but man, I know this is God. It's all a part of His plan for my life. Maxine is not a fly-by-night chick. Don't act like you've forgotten about how she and I first met."

"Yeah, I remember. You said you met her at Nordstrom. Dude, you gave her a thousand dollar gift card. Any woman would be excited about that."

"Come on, man. She didn't know how much money was on that card. Besides, I thought I was blessing a random stranger. I didn't think I'd see her anymore. Then of all the places in Chicago, shoot, in the world, I could have run into her again, it was at church. Like the Holy Trinity, I ran into her a third time coming out of a restaurant where I was about to have lunch with Pastor Scott. It doesn't get any plainer than that."

"I'll agree it's a little different, but it's still not enough to warrant a marriage proposal."

"I'm enjoying spending time with her and getting to know her. The more we're together or talking on the phone, the more I want to be with her. She's more than a pretty face. Besides, I haven't proposed yet."

"Obviously," Zachariah said, pointing at the ring sitting on the table. "But clearly you plan to."

"Only when God gives me the go ahead. I want it to be special."

Zachariah twisted the cap on a bottle of Dr. Pepper and took a long swig. "Man, I don't know about this. It feels like you're rushing into something. I don't want you to get hurt."

"Don't worry about me, bruh. I got this. You'll see when I have that fine woman on my arm. I know Maxine Miller is my future first lady."

"Oh, so now you plan to be a pastor too? I guess God gave you a sign about that, huh?"

Eli stood and retrieved the ring box from the table. A loud clap echoed throughout the room as he snapped it closed and placed the small box inside his pocket. "I see you got jokes. Any minister of the gospel worth his salt should desire to pastor one day. Otherwise, what are we doing? I don't know about you, but I have no intention of sitting under Pastor Scott for the rest of my life."

With three big gulps, Zachariah finished his beverage and expelled a loud belch. "See, that's how we're different. I have no desire to pastor a church. A lot of these cats think pastoring is cool, but I know better. Babysitting a bunch of hard-headed grown folks is not for me. I'm cool with preaching a message now and then and visiting a few members in the hospital."

"Zach, you have got to be kidding me. I can't believe you're even a minister. You make ministry sound like a job and not the call of God on your life."

"Look, man. Don't judge me. For me, ministry is not a job because I don't get paid. It's more like community service, which is different. However, there is one major similarity. When I clock out and leave work, I don't expect to be contacted until I clock back in. The same is for the church. When I leave service, I don't want people calling me to fix their problems. That's for Jesus to do. People put too much on pastors, anyway. Most of the people in churches would rather call and bug the pastor than to pray for themselves. Some of them ain't gone listen to either one, the pastor or God. It's a shame. Folks better learn how to pray for themselves, because if they're waiting on me, they better hope it's during regular service times."

"Man, you're crazy, but I can't argue with you. People need to learn to depend on God, not man. Despite the things you pointed out, I'll stand on what I know to be true. I will fulfill my call as a pastor, just like I will fulfill my duty as Maxine's husband."

Zachariah stood with Eli. "How about we finish this conversation while I dominate you in a game of pool? This ditch you're in here digging is getting too deep. If I don't give you something else to focus on, it'll be deep enough for burial."

The friends made their way to Eli's game room where he had a pool table, an indoor basketball arcade game, and a dartboard. Eli picked up the remote and turned on the 88-inch wall mounted television. The Chicago Cubs were at the top of the fifth inning, leading the St. Louis Cardinals by two runs.

Rubbing his hands together, Zachariah retrieved two cans of Red Bull from the bar area and tossed one over to Eli. "Rack 'em."

Eli prepared the pool table and stood back, allowing Zachariah room for the break shot. He watched as Zach took aim and sent the cue ball barreling into the other balls.

"You better enjoy this while you can if you plan on getting

married," Zachariah teased. "A lot of women don't like their husbands hanging around playing games."

"Here you go." Eli forced out a breath. "Just play the game. I'm not in the mood to keep hearing you sing the same song. I'm surprised you're giving me such a hard time about this. You've been married for I don't know how long. You act like you're the only one that can have a beautiful wife."

"I've been married for five years now. That's why I'm trying to get you to think about this decision. Once you're in it, it's not easy to get out. Marriage is hard, even when you've known the woman for years, like I have my wife. It's going to be much harder marrying a woman you've only known about four or five months. You're a smart man, Eli. I just hope you know what you're doing."

With expert precision, Eli knocked two striped pool balls into the corner pocket. "How about you focus on getting whooped at pool and leave figuring out my life to me?"

Seventeen

MAXINE LEANED INTO THE FLOOR-TO-CEILING MIRROR outside the office suite and touched up her lipstick. Admiring her selection of a hot pink, off the shoulder, peplum blouse and knee-length navy and pink floral pencil skirt, she tugged on her shirt in the middle, further exposing her cleavage. Four-inch navy heels gave her the perfect lift, showing off her well-toned legs. Placing the lipstick back inside her navy clutch bag, she turned and headed toward the office. It was time for her to smooth things out with Jonathan.

Stepping into the offices of Freeman, Reynolds, and Associates, Maxine left a trail of the essence from her perfume.

"Good morning," Maxine greeted her coworkers as she sashayed to her desk. Drawing closer to her desk, she noticed the desk vacated by a retired coworker was now occupied by an unknown woman. She assessed the curvy young woman before taking a seat.

A beautiful pink rose and lily bouquet sat in the middle of her desk. Maxine smiled broadly. With quick steps, she made it to her desk, bent over, and filled her lungs with the fragrant floral notes.

Seeing the flowers, Maxine reasoned, making up with Jonathan wouldn't be hard after all. He'd always sent her flowers after a disagreement, and this time was no different. Plopping down in her chair, she grasped the card and read the short note. Her eyes widened when she saw the name on the signature line was that of Eli and not Jonathan. When possible, Maxine knew she needed to stash the flowers in the ladies' room. Her saving grace was the fact Jonathan rarely came to the area where the clerks and paralegals worked. Seeing the flowers was unlikely.

"Let's see what we have going on today." Maxine spoke to the law clerk, whose desk sat opposite of hers. She logged in to her computer and scanned emails. Noting the time, she knew Jonathan was in his morning meeting with the partners of the firm. Based on previous partner meetings, she figured they would wrap up within the hour. The meeting gave her enough time to address any immediate tasks before heading to his office.

Edna, the office manager, approached Maxine's desk with steps mimicking a march. She reminded Maxine of a soldier. Edna's face twisted into a smirk. An improvement over the bitter looks she often greeted Maxine with. Edna stood in front of Maxine's desk and spoke louder than necessary.

"Maxine, the director of personnel has requested to see you in his office. Please log off and follow me."

Taken aback, Maxine peered around the room to see how many of her coworkers were watching the exchange. Not to be outdone, she replied sharply, "What does he want, and why would I follow you to an office that I clearly know how to get to?"

"What he wants is not for me to say. Now please, log off and follow me." Edna stepped away, leaving no room for a rebuttal.

"Ugh," Maxine murmured loud enough for Edna to hear her. She reluctantly complied and shuffled past Edna, sauntering to the personnel director's office. Edna's actions unnerved Maxine to no end. Maxine's relationship with Jonathan afforded her a drama free work environment, but Edna had always shown resentment toward her for the obvious favor Maxine received.

"Hey, Louie, what's up?" Maxine asked, addressing Lewis Bradshaw, the personnel director, by the nickname she had given him after beginning her employment at the firm.

"Ms. Miller, please close the door and take a seat," Lewis replied in a direct, authoritative tone.

Crossing her legs, Maxine folded her hands and placed them on her knee. "What's this about?" she asked, matching his energy.

Lewis pulled a manila folder from his desk drawer and flipped through the pages. He vigorously rubbed his chin and read over the slips of paper. He cleared his throat and loosened his necktie. "Ms. Miller, I requested this meeting with you because of some unsettling information I received this morning. Do you recall preparing documents for the Jones versus Simon Inc. case?"

"Vaguely. Why?" Maxine asked, sitting up straighter in her seat.

"The documents were prepared incorrectly. You omitted substantial information resulting in a loss exceeding eighty million dollars. As a result, the client has filed a suit against the firm, citing negligence on our part."

"That's ridiculous. I always double check my work. There is no way I submitted documents with such errors."

"I understand your desire to argue your point. However, the matter is settled. I must relieve you of your position here. Because of the enormity of the error, your termination is effective immediately. There is no offer of a severance package. You may return to your desk to retrieve your belongings under the supervision of the office manager, after which we will escort you from the office."

With a single sweep of her arm, papers shifted on Lewis's desk, followed by a crash from Maxine's chair as she stood. "This is ridiculous. Where is Mr. Freeman? I need to talk to him. You will not get away with this."

Lewis clasped his hands. His eyes bore into Maxine. "Mr. Freeman, along with the other partners, are aware of the situation. Speaking with him is not an option."

She opened her mouth, but words escaped her. Maxine couldn't believe this was happening. She knew Jonathan was upset but this was over the top, even for him. Exiting Lewis's office, Maxine found Edna standing outside with a satisfied grin plastered on her face. She returned to her desk and grabbed her handbag. Marching past Edna, she whispered a string of expletives.

Edna continued on Maxine's heels until she was outside the office. Once Maxine stood at the elevator, Edna turned and walked away, escaping behind the large polished wooden door.

With rapid taps, Maxine pressed the elevator button. The elevator door opened, and Jonathan stepped out. Pushing him back inside, Maxine pressed the button to close the door.

"What are you doing, Jonathan? I knew you were pissed when you left my house the other day, but this is crazy. You're upset about Eli, but it's not even what you think. I wanted to explain, but you wouldn't answer my calls. I was coming to talk to you after your morning meeting. Instead of hearing me out, I'm fired. Are you freaking kidding me?"

Jonathan expelled a sadistic laugh. "You must have forgotten who I am, Maxine. I told you when I left the other day you would beg me back. Look at you, you're pathetic. Firing you is only the beginning of the pain I plan to inflict on you. When I get finished with you, you'll regret the day you were born. Step aside so I can get off this elevator. I can't stand the sight of you. Oh yeah, I checked out your little preacher man. You're so stupid. I'm a billionaire, baby. He can never do for you what I've done. I guess this explains your recent trips to church. You made your bed, now lie in it. Just not in my condo."

"That's my condo. My name is on the deed. I made sure of it. Have you forgotten I was at the closing? I signed the papers."

Jonathan laughed louder. "You thought that was real? No, sweetheart, I set all that up. You were so caught up in the moment, you didn't read a thing. Instead, you bounced in your seat and giggled, asking where do you sign. You have no legal rights to my condo. I guess you better call Eli. It seems you think you have a Boaz, as they say in the church world. Nah, baby, all you got is a fat car dealer."

Maxine pressed the button, and the elevator door opened. "He may not be a Boaz, but at least he ain't Yoaz. Go straight to hell, Jonathan."

"With pleasure," he replied and stepped off the elevator. The sound of Jonathan's laughter could still be heard even after the elevator doors closed.

Eighteen

FURY COURSED THROUGH MAXINE'S VEINS LIKE LAVA. She couldn't believe the audacity of Jonathan, treating her like street trash. Maxine drove aimlessly, arriving at her building faster than usual. The smirk on Edna's face and the sound of Jonathan's laughter played in her mind like a movie on repeat. In her frustration, she arrived at the condo, but couldn't even recall driving home. The nerve of Jonathan not only having her fired, but to insinuate her home didn't belong to her was ridiculous.

Mentally exhausted, Maxine made her way to the elevator and pressed the button for the eighteenth floor. Her feet throbbed. She wanted to kick her shoes off and walk barefoot to her condo, but there was no way she would allow herself to be out in public looking less than stellar. God forbid if someone should see her, she would never live that down. With a subtle bounce, the elevator eased to a stop. Maxine trudged down the hall with her key in hand.

The minute she got inside and relieved herself of the skintight outfit and the shoes that were killing her feet, she planned to go online to the Cook County clerk's website and check the deed recording for her condo. There was no way Jonathan staged the closing, she reasoned. He wouldn't go that far, would he?

Arriving at her door, she inserted the key and turned.

"What the...?" Maxine forced the key into the lock, wiggling ferociously. For the first time, she noticed an envelope wedged into the side of the door. Maxine grabbed the envelope and ripped it open. A small key fell out, along with a folded slip of paper. Unfolding the paper, Maxine recognized Jonathan's handwriting. She read the note in disbelief.

In case you're wondering why your key isn't working, it's because I changed the locks. You can find your rags and other crap in storage unit number 304 at We Store on eighty-fifth and Ashland. Remember Maxine, I hold the cards. Without me, you have nothing.

The paper slipped from Maxine's fingers. Her hands shook with uncontrollable intensity. The entire day felt like a nightmare. Her first instinct was to call Jonathan and curse him out, but she knew that wouldn't do any good. Not only had he locked her out of her home, but he had the nerve to store her belongings at a storage unit in the hood. She wouldn't take his abuse laying down. Maxine didn't know how, but she would make Jonathan pay. Before she could plan her attack, she needed to find a hotel for the night and a comfortable outfit.

Maxine stepped out of the shower and examined her hotel room. She hadn't stayed overnight in a room that small since she was in college. She questioned her decision to go with a standard room at the upscale hotel as opposed to a suite. The space felt cramped. Checking in without a reservation had been taxing enough. After the fiasco of going through four credit cards before settling on her personal debit card, room selection was the last thing on her mind. After leaving the condo, Maxine purchased a few outfits and shoes to tide her over until she could get to the storage unit. She used the balance on the gift card she received from Eli to pay. With everything else Jonathan had done to her, him cancelling her credit cards was the last thing on her mind.

The day was filled with one disappointment after the next. She was not a weak woman, but with so much happening so fast, it was overwhelming. Maxine sat on the bed and powered on the television. Using her phone, she logged into her bank's website and checked her accounts. Her balance was enough to get her started, but there was no way it would support her lifestyle long term. She wasn't interested in securing employment right away, so she knew she would have to move fast. With Jonathan dismissing her, she needed to secure her future. A commercial for a car dealership came on the television, and Maxine displayed a devious grin. It was time to cash in her meal ticket...Eli.

Eli spent the day thinking about Maxine and praying. He hadn't received a phone call or text from her in a few days. He had become accustomed to their daily chats. Not hearing from her seemed odd. Eli received a text notification showing the flowers he sent to her job were delivered on Monday, but she hadn't acknowledged receiving them. He didn't want to seem pushy, so he resisted the urge to contact her Monday evening. It was now Thursday. Eli had an uneasy feeling that he couldn't shake. He prayed Maxine was okay.

A slight vibration emanated from the cellphone on Eli's hip, followed by a ding. He pulled the phone from its holster and viewed the message.

> Zachariah: Hey, man, I know I gave you a hard time about Maxine. I apologize. I support whatever decision you make.

> Eli: Thanks man.

Eli was glad to see his best friend was coming around. The weekend was approaching, and he wanted to take Maxine out on his boat. The only way to do so would be to call her. He thought of inviting Zachariah and his wife along but reconsidered. Based on their previous interactions, Eli knew he needed to give Maxine adequate notice for outings. Adding another couple to the mix could create unnecessary tension. The last thing he wanted to do was make her feel uncomfortable.

Thoughts of the engagement ring sitting inside his wall safe weighed heavily on his heart. He was certain Maxine was the woman for him. Since meeting her, Eli often laid in bed at night, longing to have her next to him. He tried to imagine life with her. Since they both enjoyed traveling, he thought of trips they could take to exotic locations. *Does she want children? If so, how many?* The constant thoughts of Maxine were overwhelming. There could be no more delays. Eli decided it was time for him to make Maxine his, no matter what it would take. He was determined to impress her. What better way, he reasoned, than sharing information about his wealth? She needed to know he could take care of her.

Pulling the phone from its holster, Eli called her. The phone rang several times before she picked up. She sounded frustrated.

"Hey, Maxine. Did I catch you at a bad time?"

"No, it's fine. I'm trying to get my things moved into this storage unit. It's a lot of work and I'm already over it."

"I didn't know you were moving. I would have come to help you out. When we had brunch, you mentioned wanting a larger place, but I didn't know you were already acquiring one."

"I guess that's why the saying goes, be careful what you ask for. The move wasn't planned. My condo flooded when a pipe burst. The damage was so extensive I had to leave. I've been staying in a hotel." The lies rolled off Maxine's tongue so easily she impressed herself. Maxine revealed her living situation to Eli to gauge his level of concern and commitment to her.

"Wait, you're staying in a hotel? Why didn't you call me? I mean, I'm sure it's a nice hotel, but you deserve so much better than that. How long have you been in the hotel?"

"Since Monday evening. I would've called you, but things have been crazy. Between the condo and my job situation, it was too much." Maxine purred into the phone. She tried to sound pitiful.

"Job situation? Sweetheart, it sounds like you've been going through hell."

Eli paused, pondering a thought. He'd been praying for a sign, and now he had one. Things couldn't get any clearer. Maxine needed him. The issues she mentioned were things he could fix with no effort. He was taught as a husband it would be his responsibility to provide shelter for his wife and take care of her financial needs. Eli reasoned, this had to be God answering his prayers.

"Maxine," he began, "I'm sorry you're going through all of this. I want to help you. Perhaps you can stay with me."

"Stay with you? Uh, preacher man, isn't that against what the Bible says?"

"Yes, it is. Let me start again because my offer didn't come out right. I have a guesthouse on my property. It's furnished and would offer you more space and comfort than a hotel room. You'll have your privacy and access to the main house when you want."

"Are you serious?" Maxine paused as if she were pondering the thought. "How much is this going to cost me? I'm looking for another job, so right now I'm using my savings for everything. I can't take on any more expenses."

"Sweetheart, it won't cost you a thing. I want to help you out. This isn't something I would normally do. I'm offering you the guesthouse because you need a suitable place to stay. I can provide that, so why not? Look, I'm not afraid to admit, I like you a lot. Things between us seem to be moving toward a relationship. I want to explore it."

"Eli, I don't know. This seems like a lot." Maxine feigned innocence. Eli was playing right into her hands. If this man had a yacht and a guesthouse on his property, he was either a better liar than she was, or he was selling cars to half of Chicago. Either way, she would see for herself.

"Tell you what," Eli said, cutting into Maxine's thoughts. "Why don't you come by this evening after you get settled? We can have dinner and talk. If you decide you want to stay, you're welcome to do so. If you choose not to stay, I won't be offended."

Maxine took a deep breath and released it audibly. She wanted him to think she was wrestling with the decision. "Okay, fine, Eli. Text me the address. I'll let you know when I'm finished here."

Nineteen

"GUESS WHERE I AM RIGHT NOW?" MAXINE SQUEALED into the phone.

"Maxine, please. I haven't heard from you in how long and you're calling me with riddles?"

"Girl, just do it." Maxine said, with a twinge of irritation in her voice. "Guess where I am right now."

Matching her tone, Rashida replied, "I don't know. Knowing you, you could be anywhere. I don't have time for this. It's late and I'm tired."

"Fine, I'll tell you. I'm currently stretched out on the softest king size bed I have ever laid in, which happens to be in Eli's house."

"What? I know you're lying," Rashida yelped.

"No. I'm not lying. I would video call you, but at this hour I'm sure you're not decent with your little nasty self."

"Oh my God, forget you. Girl, what are you doing in his house? Why aren't you at home?"

Maxine blew out a breath. "It's Eli's guesthouse. I'm here because I don't have a home anymore. Turns out, I never owned the condo. It was all some elaborate scheme Jonathan cooked up. Can you believe it? He set up a fake loan closing and everything. After he found out I was seeing Eli, he had me fired, then he locked me out of the condo."

"Ooh. That's messed up. Please tell me you're lying."

Maxine squinted and pulled the phone away from her ear in response to Rashida's shrill. "I wish I was. I'm the one going through it, and I can't believe it myself."

"Dang, girl. I hate to say I told you so."

"Then don't, because I swear I don't feel like hearing it. I'm going through enough as it is. I don't need you coming down on me too."

"No, hear me out. I knew Jonathan would be upset. Men think they can do whatever they want, but the moment a woman starts seeing another man, they feel violated. I knew Jonathan would do something, but I didn't know he would take it this far."

Maxine recounted the details of her job termination and eviction. She was still in disbelief that Jonathan would be so callous. She'd invested so much time in him only to have him throw her out like trash.

"I wouldn't be surprised if Jonathan moved his new side chick right up into your condo."

"I still can't believe he started seeing another woman. She must be something for him to choose her over me. The nerve of him. How does she look? Describe her."

"When I saw her, she had a short, cropped haircut. Her skin is a medium brown, you know, not light but also not very dark. She's a bit on the curvy side but cute enough, I guess."

Maxine was quiet for a few beats. "Curvy, huh? Things are making more sense. The day Jonathan had me fired, I noticed a new girl working at the firm. She was curvy and close to what you described. It could be a coincidence, but it seems odd. Especially because when the last employee vacated the position, we were told it wouldn't be filled. The timing of everything seems very suspicious."

"I agree it's weird, but like you said, it could just be a coincidence. As for you not believing he would see another woman other than you, you can get over that. Once a cheater, always a cheater. If he'll cheat with you, he will most definitely cheat on you." Rashida shifted the conversation. "Anyway, enough about Jonathan. Tell me how you ended up in Eli's guesthouse."

Cackling, Maxine perked up. "When Jonathan evicted me from the condo, he put all my stuff in a storage unit on Ashland. With nowhere to go, I was staying at a hotel. Earlier today, I hired some movers to take my belongings from the storage unit Jonathan rented to one more suitable for my taste. Eli called me while I was moving my stuff. You know from the beginning, my plan was to marry a preacher. I figured now is as good of a time as any, so I tested him."

"How did you test him?" Rashida asked.

"I told him my condo flooded, and I lost my job. Girl, I expected him to offer to put me up in a better hotel or something. That's when he shocked me by telling me I could stay in his guesthouse. Mind you, I had never been to his house, so I didn't know what he was working with. Not long ago, he mentioned owning a yacht. I knew he had some money, but when I saw his house, my mind was blown. This house is gorgeous and huge. I asked him why he bought such a big house. He told me he wanted a place that would be large enough for his future wife and kids."

"Kids? How will that work? You do know how babies are made, right?"

"Be for real, Rashida. I might want children. I haven't decided yet, but that's beside the point. Can we dwell on the fact that I'm at Eli's home? Well, guesthouse, but pretty much the same thing."

"I'm not trying to get all up in your business, but if you

needed somewhere to stay, why didn't you call me or go to your mother's house?"

Pondering Rashida's statement, Maxine thought for a moment. Calling Rashida was not an option because Maxine wasn't willing to spend one night at Rashida's place. When they went places together, if she was driving, she only did so during the day. She was never comfortable driving her Maserati in Rashida's neighborhood. As for her mother, they still hadn't attempted to repair their relationship. Her mother, Rose, had informed Maxine she would not accept her relationship with a married man under any uncertain terms. Maxine hadn't spoken to her mother since the day she called and blasted her for telling Maxwell's mother her business.

"I didn't call either of you because I got this. Can't you see? My plan is falling into place. Mark my words, Eli will propose to me before you can blink. I guarantee it."

Twenty

Eli descended the stairs, drawn by the enticing aromas of bacon, eggs, pancakes and coffee. He found Maxine singing in the kitchen as she prepared breakfast. His eyes roamed her body, admiring the striped pajama shorts she wore that stopped just below her buttocks. As he approached, she turned and greeted him, revealing a V-neck pajama top that teased his eyes.

"Good morning, Eli," she greeted. Approaching, she wrapped her arms around him and kissed his cheek. "Come on, have a seat. I fixed you breakfast."

Maxine grabbed Eli's hand and led him to the dining table. The smell of her perfume was intoxicating, even with the aroma of pancakes and warm syrup wafting through the air.

For the past three weeks, Maxine had spent as much time in Eli's house as she had at the guesthouse. It startled him the first time he came home and found her inside the house. Although he had been involved in relationships in the past, none of the women had the free rein of his home that he afforded Maxine. Their time together was invaluable. Having Maxine so close gave Eli the experience of cohabitation without the intimacy.

After the first week and a half of living on Eli's property, Maxine started coming to the main house dressed relaxed. She'd worn pajamas a few times when she joined him for movies in the home theater. Never anything as revealing as her current choice.

Eli was a Christian man, and he loved the Lord, but he wasn't perfect. Her appearance was tempting him to a point of discomfort, but he didn't want her to stop. He wanted more. Eli reasoned if he was going to maintain a good standing with the Lord, he would have to move forward with his plans of making Maxine his wife.

"Everything looks and smells delicious, sweetheart. I'll never drop this weight if you keep preparing meals like this." Eli chuckled before adding pancake, eggs, and a piece of bacon to his fork. He wanted to experience each of the components of the meal in one bite.

Maxine stood and walked behind Eli's chair, massaging his shoulders. "I guess we'll have to find a way to work it off," she whispered into his ear.

Eli coughed, nearly choking on a piece of bacon he popped into his mouth.

"Are you okay?" Maxine asked, patting him hard in the middle of his back.

"I'm fine," Eli replied, leaning over to avoid another blow. "My goodness woman, you are heavy-handed."

"Oops, I'm sorry. You scared me. I wasn't about to have you in here dying on me."

He laughed, causing him to cough again. Eli picked up his glass and took a sip of orange juice. "Sweetheart, I'm not going anywhere. What can I say? You caught me off guard. I may be saved, but I'm not dead. Having a beautiful woman whispering in my ear almost took me there."

Pushing her chair away from the table with his foot, Eli beckoned for Maxine to take a seat. She complied and directed her attention back to her food.

"I didn't mean to make you uncomfortable. You've been so great since I've been here. I wanted to do something nice for you. I can see how my actions came across as seductive. Just so you know, I was referring to us making use of all that fitness equipment you have in your home gym. This property and neighborhood are perfect for a workout outside as well."

"You're right." Eli took another bite of food. "I bought that equipment with the best intentions. I use it sometimes. Obviously not often enough." He patted his stomach. "Running the dealership takes a lot out of me."

Maxine stared into his eyes. "Eli, you are a wonderful man, so I'm going to tell you straight up. You can make excuses, or you can make it happen. It boils down to desire. When you want something, you go for it." She extended her arms and looked around the room. "This happens when desire meets effort. Unless you're involved in some serious illegal activity, I'm guessing you didn't accumulate all you have by happenstance."

Eli eyed Maxine. He considered sharing the details of his father's lottery win, but determined he was better off reserving that information. Maxine was proving to not only be who he wanted, she was the woman he needed in his life.

"Why are you looking at me like that? Did I offend you or something?"

"Not at all. I was thinking. You've been cooped up in this house so much. Perhaps we should get away. What do you think about spending the weekend on the water?"

Maxine jumped up from her chair and threw her arms around Eli. She plastered him with kisses, being careful to avoid his lips.

"I take it your answer is yes." Laughing, Eli pushed back from the table. "I need to make a phone call to get everything set up.

Why don't you go pack a bag? I'll call you with the details of when we'll leave."

With one last embrace, Maxine pranced toward the guesthouse.

Eli went to his bedroom and called Liam, the yacht's captain. Eli hired Liam immediately after he acquired the Cayman. Liam headed the three-person crew. They employed Daliah as the chef after the first voyage. Eli realized he didn't want to prepare his own meals on the boat after having to do so on his first voyage. Brandon served as the vessel's steward.

The crew remained on Eli's payroll eight months out of the year. They were contracted to be on call, allowing Eli to take spontaneous trips with minimal effort.

Everything Eli prayed for seemed to line up. Business at the dealership had been on a steady incline for the last two quarters. New car sales had doubled, with the sales team pushing to close deals. The incentive program and friendly competition kept the sales staff motivated.

Watching Maxine maneuver around his kitchen made Eli desire her even more than he had before. He knew it was risky inviting Maxine to live on his property. To ease the conviction he felt, Eli reasoned he couldn't with a good conscience allow her to live in a hotel room when he had more space than he could fill alone. It seemed the more he prayed for signs, the more Maxine's actions proved she was the answer to his prayers. Since moving in, Maxine had become more affectionate. She often greeted him with warm hugs and snuggled up next to him during movies.

Eli saw Maxine as wife material. He hoped the weekend trip he planned would reveal where he stood with her. Either she would agree to take their relationship further, or he'd have to accept permanent placement in the friend zone.

Twenty-One

Belmont Harbor was abuzz. Boats and yachts of all shapes and sizes were docked. There appeared to be as many boaters coming in as there were going out. Eli parked his vehicle and grabbed their bags from the trunk. He stiffened in surprise when Maxine enveloped her arms around his arm. It felt good having a woman by his side. The couple approached the yacht and saw Liam waiting to greet them.

"Wow, this boat is beautiful," Maxine complimented. "What does Migdal-Ōz mean?" she asked, pointing to the name painted on the stern of the vessel.

"It's a Hebrew name meaning strong tower," Eli said. "Look at that structure. Doesn't she look strong?"

"Ah, strong tower." Maxine nodded. "I like that. Something about it makes me feel secure."

"As you should, my dear. Shall we?" Eli beckoned towards the yacht and they stepped aboard. He introduced her to the crew. Starting with Liam, the captain, then the chef, Daliah. "This woman will have your taste buds dancing. She is an amazing chef." Lastly, he introduced her to Brandon and handed him their bags.

Eli was eager to give Maxine a tour of the yacht. Starting with the sleeping quarters, he showed her the room where she would sleep, followed by his room. From there, he ushered her to the dining area and interior lounging space. Once they made it to the deck and reclined, Daliah handed them each a glass of Sangria.

Liam approached. "Mr. Clayton, all systems are a go. Are you ready to set sail, sir?"

"Yes! Let's do it."

The weather was perfect for sailing. Maxine came dressed for a day on the water. Her powder blue blouse danced as the wind flowed through the loose fitting fabric. White linen shorts stopped in the middle of Maxine's thigh. The gladiator sandals she wore revealed perfectly pedicured feet. Powder blue polish glistened on her fingernails and toes. The large floppy hat she wore shielded her face from the sun.

Eli observed Maxine as she reclined and sipped her sangria. She was so beautiful. He wanted so badly to touch her. Eli stood and walked to the bow of the vessel. He looked out at the water and the clear sky. In his heart, he prayed. *Lord, I'm struggling here. I want to do what is right, but I'm a man. My desire for this woman is so strong. I believe you sent her to me. Please be with me as I make decisions that will affect the rest of my life.*

Maxine walked up behind him and wrapped her arms around his belly. She snuggled against his back. "Thank you for this trip. The water is so relaxing. I didn't realize how stressed I was until I got out here. I don't know what it is, but it's something special about being out here, away from the noise of the city. A girl could get used to this. I'm a city girl to the core, but this has a different vibe. I like it."

"I know what you mean. When I need to get away from it all,

I often find myself out here on the water. I turn my phone off and leave my computer and tablet at home."

Releasing Eli, Maxine asked, "How can you disconnect so completely? Don't you worry about missing an emergency call or something?"

Eli turned and faced her. "No, I don't. I used to be the type to never go anywhere or do anything. I was always afraid to disconnect, thinking I would miss something, or someone would need me, and I wouldn't be there for them. What I found was I was miserable. Eventually, I came to realize I was missing out on so much, waiting for something bad to happen. As a single man, my friends and family called on me first. They figured since I wasn't married and didn't have children, I was always available. My pastor often called me when there were other men in the church capable of completing the same tasks. The point is, I had to make myself a priority."

Taking Maxine's hands into his, Eli continued. "One day, I plan to marry. I can't expect my wife to sit back while I take care of everyone else's problems. That wouldn't be fair to her or me. I realized it was better to make the changes before it becomes a problem."

Looking up, Eli curled his lips into a half smile. There was no more need for guessing games. The moment he had been waiting for had arrived. It was time to pop the question.

Twenty-Two

THE NIGHT AIR WAS COOL. WAVES CRASHED AGAINST the side of the boat in a harmonious symphony. Clear skies provided the perfect backdrop for a blanket of stars. A soft glow settled on the water, illuminated by the full moon. Maxine pulled a blanket tight around her shoulders to ward off the cutting winds. She took careful steps as she walked around the deck.

Thoughts of Jonathan invaded her mind. He had been a huge part of her life for so long. Until recently, she would have sworn he loved her as much as she loved him. Adjusting to life without him was difficult.

Maxine had to admit, the attention she received from Eli was refreshing. She never imagined he would be so wealthy. By all appearances, Eli looked like a regular guy. Had he not given her the gift card at Nordstrom, she never would have offered him a second glance. As she reflected on the way things were turning out, throwing caution to the wind had proven to be quite beneficial.

Warming up to Eli was becoming easier day by day. His personality was much more attractive than his appearance. She wanted to let her guard down and fully embrace him, but when she looked at him, she longed for Jonathan. For a man in his mid-sixties, Jonathan was in great shape. His statuesque frame was slim yet sculpted with toned muscles. His salt and pepper goatee and mustache were groomed to perfection. When he smiled, her heart melted. Maxine reminisced about rubbing his bald head.

"Sweetheart, Daliah has prepared dinner. Are you ready to eat?"

Startled, Maxine dropped her blanket and grabbed the wall to keep from stumbling. She laughed inwardly. Perhaps she was wrong for being on Eli's boat, thinking about Jonathan.

Eli reached out to steady her. "I'm sorry. I didn't mean to scare you."

"It's okay. I should have been paying attention." Maxine placed her hand on his arm and followed him to the dinner table.

Daliah had prepared the two of them a meal worthy of a Michelin star restaurant. Once Maxine was seated, Daliah removed the cloche from their dishes, revealing seared grilled tuna topped with mango papaya salsa. Crispy roasted potatoes, grilled asparagus, and sautéed anise carrots completed the meal.

Maxine couldn't believe it. She was no stranger to luxury treatments, having spent time with Jonathan, but things with Eli were distinctly different. Maxine appreciated having a man dote on her, both in private and public. She didn't know if she would ever find Eli attractive, let alone love him, but he was a means to an end. Eli wouldn't be the first man she was involved with for the benefits.

Sanford Estabar was the first married man Maxine crossed the line with. They met at an alumni fundraiser banquet held celebrating a successful corporate sponsorship. Maxine took part in a team of twelve students tasked with acquiring monies to fund a project, allowing eligible students to receive laptop computers or tablets for use throughout their college career.

Academic excellence was instilled in Maxine from childhood. Her grandmother, a powerful influence in her life, was denied the privilege of education as a child. She relied on others to teach her how to read and write. When her grandmother bore children, she vowed no one would deny her children an education. Grandma Frances worked extra hard as a domestic to ensure her children never had to work as farmhands.

Maxine's grandmother saved for three years until she could move to Chicago with her brother, Otis. Departing oppressive conditions in Muleton, Mississippi, she was able to provide her children with a full education from elementary school to college. Maxine's mother held a bachelor's degree in business administration. Her uncle preferred to attend trade school. He focused his attention on becoming a licensed HVAC contractor.

Throughout her educational career, Maxine competed for top honors. She was determined to be the top performer in any task placed before her. Her efforts paid off when she became valedictorian of her high school class, beating out 380 other students to claim the top honor. Scholarship opportunities were abundant.

Maxine accepted a scholarship from Northwestern University as a political science major. Her scholarship covered the cost of her classes, books, housing, and meals. Unfortunately for Maxine, the fund didn't have budgetary room for extras.

Sanford approached Maxine and introduced himself as the team mingled with potential donors. He complimented her on the work her team had accomplished.

"You're much too beautiful to be working so hard. You need to focus on your studies." Sanford reached into his wallet and pulled out a business card. He presented Maxine with the card and invited her to meet with him at his office the following day.

Accepting the card, Maxine ran her fingers across the engraved letters that spelled out Estabar Holdings. With a gentle pat on her arm, Sanford bowed his head and stepped away. Maxine struggled to sleep that night. She didn't know what the meeting with Sanford would entail, but she was optimistic. She was attending school on scholarship and her grades were good, so she figured he couldn't do anything to hinder her education.

Maxine arrived at the fifteen story building at twelve forty-five. She looked up at the tower and her stomach turned in knots. She fidgeted with her hands, twirling her thumbs. The rapid beat of her heart rang in her ears. Entering the elevator, beads of sweat formed on her brow. Maxine pressed the button for the thirteenth floor. The ride up was swift.

With a slight bounce, the elevator came to a halt. The doors parted, revealing an exquisite office suite. A large cherry wood executive desk sat opposite the elevator. Maxine admired the serene waterfall fountain on the right wall. Burgundy, pleated leather wingback chairs with polished cherry wood legs sat on each side of the fountain.

A man who introduced himself as Sanford Estabar's assistant approached Maxine with a smile. "Miss Miller, I presume?" he said, in place of a greeting.

Maxine nodded.

"Mr. Estabar is expecting you. Please follow me."

The assistant crossed the room and tapped on Sanford's office door. He turned the knob and walked inside without waiting for a response. Maxine followed close behind with short, swift steps that resembled more of a trot than a sophisticated walk. Halting in front of Sanford's desk, she awaited further instruction.

Sanford extended his hand toward a set of chairs in front of his desk. He relaxed, leaning back in his chair and created a triangle with his hands. "Miss Miller, please have a seat."

"Thank you for accepting the invitation to meet with me today." His piercing glance boldly scanned Maxine's body. "Congratulations on exceeding your goal at last night's fundraiser. I'm told it was one of the most successful events the school has sponsored."

"Thank you, Mr. Estabar. Our team worked hard preparing for the event."

Sanford raised his hands, halting her speech. "No need to be so formal, Miss Miller. As a proud Alum of Northwestern University, I attend several events throughout the year. On rare occasions, I find a student I'm willing to invest in. Most of the students I have worked with in the past pursued degrees in my line of work." He reached into his desk and pulled out a thick envelope and extended it to Maxine.

Maxine moved to accept the envelope. Sanford gazed into her eyes and tightened his grip. She pulled her hand back and tilted her head.

"I don't understand. You extended the envelope as if you were giving it to me, but now you won't let it go. What kind of game are you playing?" Maxine crossed her arms in defiance.

"There's no game, Miss Miller. The contents of this envelope belong to you whether or not you choose to accept my offer. Allow me to explain." Sanford sat the envelope down on his desk. He leaned back in his chair and continued, "You see, I've done my homework. You attend Northwestern on scholarship, do you not?"

"Yes, but what does that have to do with anything?"

"Pick up the envelope, Miss Miller."

Maxine obeyed, pulling the envelope close. She looked inside. Her mouth fell open as she ran her fingers across the strap of twenty-dollar bills. Frown lines appeared between her eyebrows. "What's this?"

"Hmm," Sanford clasped his hands together and pressed his index fingers against his lips. "Like I said before, on rare occasions I find a special student. Since your major is Political Science, I can't take you under my wing as a mentee. I'll have to help you in other ways."

"What do you mean by 'other ways'?"

"According to my research, Miss Miller, it appears you could use some additional funding outside of your scholarship. Monies that could make college easier for you. In that envelope you're holding is simply put, help. If it makes you feel better, we can call it a scholarship."

"Is that so?" Maxine shot back. "What do you expect in return for this?" Maxine raised her hands and made air quotes before continuing, "scholarship, as you call it."

"Not much," Sanford said, "just a bit of appreciation now and then. If you know what I mean. Oh, and Miss Miller, we will need to keep our interactions confidential."

Maxine shuddered at the thought of Sanford. She'd spent her entire college career showing Sanford Estabar her appreciation with intimate acts. If she could endure Sanford, a man old enough to be her grandfather, Eli was a piece of cake.

Twenty-Three

"Sweetheart, are you okay?" Eli asked, placing his fork on the table.

"Huh?" Maxine replied, shaking her head as if she were trying to wake herself. "I'm fine. Why would you think otherwise?"

"You kind of zoned out on me for a moment. It looks like you were deep in thought."

"It's nothing, Eli. I'm good. What were you saying?" Maxine turned her attention to her food.

Eli eyed Maxine suspiciously. He decided it was best to let it go. The ring box felt like a paperweight in his pocket. The weight of the box was nothing compared to the weight of his thoughts. He was prepared to put himself out there, but the realization she could say no gave him pause. If she said no, it would make the rest of the trip awkward.

Eli struggled to pull Maxine back into the moment. Whatever she had on her mind seemed heavy. "Daliah, did an excellent job on this meal. These potatoes are delicious."

"Yeah. It's good."

Dinner wasn't going the way Eli wanted. He was trying to set the stage for a romantic proposal, but Maxine seemed disconnected from the moment. Eli acknowledged he knew little about her, but in the time he spent with her, he knew there was one subject Maxine always responded to. He shifted the conversation.

"Are you enjoying being out here on the water? Is the boat to your liking?"

"I am. The experience has been pleasurable." Maxine looked up and smiled. "I've been on cruise ships before, but never on a yacht. I wasn't sure what to expect, but I'm very pleased." Placing her napkin on the table, she gave Eli her full attention. "This is a nice size boat. You own this?"

"I do. It was a gift from my father. He and my mother enjoy boating as much as I do. My father knew I was in the market for a boat. I had talked about it for years. He presented this baby to me as a gift on my thirty-fifth birthday."

"Oh, so you have that generational wealth going on, I see. I'm not mad at you. That's a blessing. Especially to see it in our community." Maxine relaxed her shoulders. "Do you have siblings? I can't believe I never asked before."

Eli wasn't lost on Maxine's comment about his family's wealth. It didn't matter to him. The money he received from his father admittedly placed him far ahead of his peers, however sound business decisions had allowed him to accumulate significant wealth on his own.

"I have a brother. He's eight years younger than me, but we keep in close touch even though he's rarely in the Chicago area. What about you?"

"Nope, just me. My mother said she didn't want to spend her life tied to raising a bunch of children. She got pregnant with me in her junior year of college. My grandmother helped raise me so my mother's education wasn't compromised. My mother maintained employment my entire childhood. If it hadn't been for my grandmother, I would have been a latchkey kid. Once I went to college, my mother focused on herself. I can't say I blame her. Shortly after I graduated from college, she met my stepfather. He has been a big part of my life since. Pops never treated me like I was an outside child, even though I was grown when they married. My mother is such a strong woman. They have been married over ten years, but she's still super independent."

"That must be where you get your independence from."

"Yep. I guess I get it from both my mother and grandmother. I come from a line of strong, independent women. Not independent to the point of saying I don't need a man. On the contrary, I hope the man God has for me is ready for me. I want a man that will love me and be able to take care of me. I'm sure you've heard the expression love don't pay the bills."

Maxine hoped Eli would get the subliminal message. She expected him to take care of her, but she was going to have her way, no matter what. If she wanted something, she would get it. If she didn't want to do something, he wouldn't change her mind. With him being a minister, she threw the God statement in for good measure.

"Yes, I'm familiar with the statement. I've heard it my whole life. My father instilled in me and my brother he was raising real men. Men who would take care of their family and themselves," Eli answered. He stood and walked over to Maxine. "Would you care to join me on the deck? It's a beautiful night. You don't see skies like this in the city. I want us to take full advantage."

"Sure, let me grab my shawl."

"Look at me. I can keep you warm. You don't have to worry about that. We also have the pontoon fire pit to ward off the night air." Eli removed his wineglass from the table and waited for Maxine to do the same. Placing his hand on her back, he gently coached her outside.

"Let's sit over here by the fire," Eli said, guiding Maxine to the lounging area. He pondered his words. There was no way he could use phrases suitable for a couple that had been dating for years. They wouldn't make sense. He also didn't want to scare her off by saying God showed him she was his wife. Eli took a sip from his glass and spoke from the heart.

"Maxine, you are so beautiful. That smile of yours could melt the coldest heart. When you first came into my life, I thought it was merely a fluke. Never in my wildest imaginations did I think we would sit here at this moment. As you know, I'm a praying man. I pray about people who enter my life. I have experienced enough to know not everyone who enters your life is meant to stay."

Eli took Maxine's hand in his. "Life is different with you. You are open about what you want in life. I love that you have your stuff together. There's nothing more unattractive to me than a woman over thirty-five who's still trying to find herself. What I know for sure is you have added so much to my life. My actions may seem odd because we haven't known each other long. Listen, I didn't achieve the level of success I have by being naïve. Life has been good. Even better since you moved into the guesthouse. You have been a friend, and a much needed and desired companion. I guess what I want to know is..." Eli pulled the box from his pocket and opened it. "Will you join me on this journey called life? I can take care of you. I know you have been looking for a job, but you don't have to. You can pursue your dream of working with women and young girls. Maxine, will you be my wife?"

Maxine stared at the exquisite square cut diamond ring in Eli's hand. She had a feeling he was moving toward solidifying their relationship. She'd hoped for a proposal, but wasn't expecting it to happen so soon. Maxine had a big fish on the line and there was no way she would let him get away.

"Oh my God, Eli," she gushed. "This is so unexpected." Maxine took a deep breath and held it. Covering her mouth with her hands, she appeared to ponder Eli's proposal. "It's so soon. Are you sure you want to marry me? We haven't known each other very long. You've never even asked me to be your girlfriend." Small lines appeared on her forehead. "Again, I ask, are you sure this is what you want?"

"Of course, I'm sure. I've never been more certain about anything. Look, this is serious business. I wouldn't play about marriage. I realize you may have some concerns, but hear me when I tell you, I'll be good to you. There is nothing within my power that I wouldn't do for you." Eli placed his hand on her cheek. "So, what do you say, Maxine Miller? Will you be my wife?"

"This is crazy," Maxine replied, shaking her hands beside her head. "I can't believe I'm saying this. I must be out of my mind, but yes, Eli, I'll marry you." Maxine extended her hand, prompting Eli to put the ring on her finger. She adjusted the ring. "It's a bit too big, but it's not a big deal. We can get it sized."

"Come here, girl," Eli said. Pulling Maxine into his arms, he kissed her passionately.

Maxine surrendered to Eli's embrace and returned the kiss with matched passion. Stretching her hand out behind his back, she gazed at the diamond ring gracing her finger. The center stone looked to be about three or four carats. She'd confirm the size once she had it appraised. The band was accented with diamonds on each side.

Relaxing his embrace, Eli attempted another kiss.

"Eli, wait." Maxine backed away from him and placed her hand on top of his. "I realize we're engaged now, but I don't want to rush things. This ring does not give you a free pass to my body. I want to wait until we're married before we become intimate."

Eli nodded. "I desire to wait as well. I would never take advantage of you. I will honor you the same as I honor God. As a minister of the gospel, I try to live my life according to the Bible. I want God to bless our union. For that to happen, I have to do things the right way."

"Good, so we agree?" Maxine asked. She wasn't interested in all the God stuff Eli was talking about. She just didn't want him putting his sloppy body on hers any sooner than he had to. One thing was certain, if he was going to be her husband, he needed to be making some changes. When they returned home, she was putting him on a diet.

Eli laid in bed, looking at the stars through the skylight of his cabin. Things had gone better than he expected with Maxine. It elated him she'd accepted his proposal. Experiencing her sweet kiss sent a warm sensation throughout his body. He told her he also wanted to wait for marriage before they became intimate. Inwardly, he was hoping for a short engagement.

Knowing Maxine was in the cabin just a few feet away from him was unnerving. He wanted her by his side. Eli could hardly wait for when he could sleep with her curled up in his arms. Maxine would never have to wonder about his feelings for her. He would make it a point to show her his love every day.

Thoughts of Maxine flooded Eli's mind. He wondered what she was thinking. Was she lying in bed thinking of him the way he was thinking of her? Was she thinking about wedding plans? She could very well be sleeping. Following the proposal, Eli had beckoned for Brandon to bring them champagne to celebrate. Maxine consumed three quarters of the bottle herself.

Once Eli and Maxine returned to the city, he would share the news of their engagement with his parents. He created scenarios for the meeting in his mind. His father, no doubt, would take one look at Maxine and slap him on the back instead of a high five. His mother, on the other hand, would do the exact opposite. She would look at Maxine and think she was after his money. Eli's mother had made the statement before with a woman he dated who was less attractive than Maxine. It unnerved him to think his mother believed he couldn't have a woman who would love him for who he was, not his assets. Once his mother got an idea in her head, it was almost impossible to change her mind. He reasoned his mother's opinion didn't matter. He knew in his heart Maxine was the woman for him.

Eli thought about his brother and chuckled. Much like their father, one look at Maxine's face and body, and he would be completely on board with the marriage. Eli was a man that could hold his own against any opposition from his family. He knew what made them tick. Maxine's family was a different story. He didn't know how they would react to her engagement following a practically nonexistent courtship. The best he could hope for was Maxine's family being supportive of their union. Either way, it would not deter him.

Twenty-Four

Maxine: FaceTime me right now!

MAXINE TEXTED AS SOON AS SHE WAS SECURE IN THE guesthouse. Emotions running rampant, she paced the floor and stared at her phone, waiting for a response.

Rashida: Give me a minute. I'm in the checkout line at the grocery store.

Maxine: Hurry up. I keep telling you to get your grocery delivered. Going to the store is outdated. One day you're going to listen to me.

Maxine moved to her closet and examined the offerings. Eli had made plans for them to visit his parents for lunch. She wanted to make a good impression. Her phone played the designated computerized ring for an incoming video call. Maxine dashed to her bed and picked up the phone. She pressed accept to answer the call.

"Darn, girl, why are you out of breath?" Rashida asked, turning up her lip.

"Because I was in the other room," Maxine replied, catching her breath. "I forgot to take my phone with me. What have you been up to?"

"Nothing."

"Ugh, that response was dry, but you know what? It doesn't even matter. I'm not letting anything get to me today. We'll get to me later. I want to hear about you. Are you still seeing Alvin?" Maxine was beaming.

Rashida furrowed her eyebrows. "Girl, why are you acting so weird?"

"What do you mean?" Maxine laughed.

"For one, you're bouncing all over the place. Plus, you're asking questions you already know the answers to. You know good and well I'm still seeing Alvin. We talked about him the other day. Why are you acting all brand new? Stop stalling. What was so important that you needed me to FaceTime you? Your text made things seem urgent. I'm on here now, and you're having a casual conversation. What's up?"

"Bam!" Maxine held her left hand up in front of her face, displaying her engagement ring.

"What's that?"

"What does it look like, Rashi? It's an engagement ring. Eli proposed."

Pursing her lips, Rashida replied, "I know you lying. If that man proposed to you already, you must have really put it on him."

"He did propose, and I didn't put nothing on him. Shoot, I never even kissed him until after I accepted his proposal." Maxine pulled the phone closer to her face. "I told you it was going to happen. A man like Eli is proud to have me on his arm. Ha, like people say all the time, won't He do it?" Closing her eyes, Maxine waved her hand in the air.

Rashida took in a breath and forced it out through her nose. "You're going to get enough of playing with God. Keep playing if you want to."

"Why are you being such a hater, Rashida? You're my girl. We have always had each other's back, no matter who we were dating or whatever. You have been tripping throughout this whole process. If you're worried about me forgetting you, don't. I got you. I'm not going to come up and not hook you up. This man has crazy money. While we were on the yacht, he told me his father bought it for him as a gift. It's a multi-million dollar boat. Eli comes from money. He only has one brother. Who do you think is going to inherit his parent's money? You can trip all you want. When it comes to Eli, I don't care what you say. I hit the jackpot with this one. Now, if you play your cards right, I might hook you up with his brother."

"Nah, that's okay. I'm good. You do you, Boo. I have my popcorn and my Coke ready. I'm going to wait and see how this plays out. You just got the ring and you're already sounding like one of those Real Housewives chicks. The only thing I have to say is you better not put me in an ugly bridesmaid's dress."

"Oh, don't worry. You won't need a dress because you won't be a bridesmaid."

"Really, Maxine. You're upset about my reaction to the point of not including me in your wedding? That's cool." Rashida rolled her eyes, making sure Maxine saw her frustration.

Maxine shook her head. "Ooh, girl. Your weave must be sewn in too tight. You are tripping for real. I'm not having any bridesmaids because I'm not having a wedding. Some women have dreamed about their wedding day since they were little girls, but that's not me. I don't want a wedding. I don't want, nor do I need, the stress of planning a wedding."

"I never knew that about you. What will you do if Eli wants a wedding?"

"He won't. When he sees how adamant I am about not having a wedding, he'll either comply or I'll pretend I will not marry him. I bet he'll straighten up then."

"You know what, to each her own. I guess there's nothing else for me to say, other than congratulations." Rashida hunched her shoulders and stared at Maxine for a moment. "Alright, girl. We need to get off this phone. I have ice cream in the car, and I've been sitting in this parking lot way too long. I'll talk to you later."

Maxine disconnected the call and placed the phone on the night table next to her. She didn't know what Rashida's problem was, but she refused to allow her to dull her shine. For some reason, her friend was acting holier than thou. She considered the possibility of Rashida being jealous. It wouldn't be the first time she displayed envy when something was going good for Maxine. Rashida eventually came around.

Worry lines creased Maxine's forehead as a tightness gripped the pit of her stomach. A small part of her felt guilty about her plans for Eli. He was a nice guy. She couldn't ignore the light in his eyes when he looked at her. Perhaps eventually, her heart would soften towards him. When she thought about it, Eli wasn't a bad looking guy. All he really needed was to lose some weight. With a little effort, she could make this work.

Returning to her closet, Maxine selected a yellow floral maxi dress with butterfly sleeves. She wanted to be conservative, but cute. The design accentuated her toned waist and hips. Maxine had never met the parents of a man she was involved with. Apart from a few casual flings, her past relationships were either not serious or the man was married.

As a future minister's wife, Maxine figured Eli's mother would expect her son to marry a more conservative woman. The gentle massage of her fingertips pressed against her temples did little to soothe the mounting stress. Maxine sat in a wingback chair opposite her bed. In a couple of hours, she'd put on the performance of a lifetime. First impressions were important. She planned to make a great one. Once the whole meet-the-parents formality was over, Maxine would start working on convincing Eli to cut this engagement short and elope.

Twenty-Five

"I DON'T THINK YOUR MOTHER LIKES ME."

"What would make you think that? Did she say something to you?" Eli picked up the TV remote and paused the movie.

Maxine snuggled closer to Eli. "She didn't say anything, per se. I mean, she didn't come right out and say I don't like you, but she was mean mugging me all afternoon. From the time we got there, and you introduced me, she had this look on her face."

"Aw, sweetheart, I'm sure you misunderstood. That's just my mom's demeanor. She's always reserved when she meets somebody new. With her facial expressions, she gets accused of frowning all the time."

Sitting up, Maxine turned to Eli. "Listen. When you announced our engagement, your father was all smiles, but not your mom. She rolled her eyes. Later, I offered to help her clear the table. She pinned me in the corner in the kitchen. She had the nerve to ask me if I was pregnant."

"She what?" Eli exclaimed.

"You heard me. She caught me so far off guard I started coughing, which made her think I was lying when I said no.

Then, she started hitting me with rapid fire questions like, how did we meet, how long have we been dating, are we sleeping together. I politely excused myself by asking if I could use the powder room. When I went in there, I cleared my head and came out to join you and your dad. I'm sure I didn't make it any better when I didn't return to the kitchen, but at that point, I was done."

Eli grabbed his forehead and shook his head. "I'm sorry, sweetheart. I didn't know she was interrogating you. She should have directed her questions to me. I would have respectfully told her to mind her business."

"If we are going to get married, I need to know our marriage is between us. I'm too old to bother myself with playing up to your mother every time I'm in her presence. I refuse to live that way." Maxine scooted further away from Eli. Peering in his eyes, she waited for his response.

Closing the distance between them, Eli grabbed Maxine's hand and kissed it above her engagement ring. "When you become my wife, nothing and no one will come before you. I honor marriage in every way. I've heard stories of how men got married and allowed their mothers to interfere in their marriage. Many of those marriages don't survive. I won't let it happen to us."

Eli's phone rang, interrupting his conversation with Maxine. He looked at the phone, stood, and stepped away from the couch, leaving Maxine alone.

"Hello, Sister Jones. How are you? Yes, I received your email. Uh, huh. That works for me. Okay, I'll see you then. Alright, you be blessed." Eli ended his phone call and returned to Maxine. He sat beside her, pulled her into his arms, and kissed her on the forehead.

"Who was that?" Maxine asked, pulling away from him. "And why did you have to go over there to take the call? Do you have another woman or something? I refuse to be second to anybody. I'm not trying to be a side chick."

"No, the call was nothing of the sort. It was Sister Jones. She's the secretary at Pastor Theodore Youngblood's church. The pastor had her email me an invitation to speak at their church. They're finalizing the schedule. She wanted to make sure I'm available. The service is next Sunday. I want you to go with me."

"The way you handled the call was not cool." Maxine pulled away. "It makes you look real suspect."

"I can see how my actions could be perceived as wrong. I'm accustomed to excusing myself when I take calls. Don't worry, I'll be more conscience from now on." Eli kissed Maxine on the forehead. "Will you go with me?"

"Yes, I'll go. But first, I need to go shopping for an outfit. I can't show up on the arm of the preacher looking crazy."

"I don't have a problem with you going shopping. I want my fiancé looking and feeling good. You can put the purchase on my credit card."

"Thank you, I will. I need to see what you have in your closet so we can coordinate." Maxine perked up. With Eli being an associate minister at his home church, he was merely a glorified member of the congregation. The speaking engagement at Pastor Youngblood's church would place the attention on him. As his fiancé, she needed to make sure the spotlight was on her.

The church was packed. Maxine watched as the congregants clapped and sang. The musicians put on a miniature concert, keeping tune with everything the pastor said. Twenty minutes into the service, the music lowered, and everyone took their seats. Pastor Youngblood introduced Eli as the guest speaker and beckoned him to step forward.

Eli stood at the podium and looked out over the congregation. The church goers were high spirited, which Eli enjoyed. His eyes fell on Maxine. The maroon and black wide brim hat she wore did nothing to mask her beauty. He felt good standing before the congregation in his black tailored suit. Maxine coordinated their outfits, purchasing a maroon shirt for him that matched her dress perfectly. She smiled, giving him the encouragement he needed to deliver the message he knew God had placed in his heart. Eli rubbed his palm over the top of his Bible then began.

"People of God, I know you're expecting me to read a scripture and expound on it, but today I'm going in a different direction."

Silence invaded the room.

"When Jesus walked the earth, he ministered the gospel by speaking in parables. Instead of a scripture, I want to share a story with you."

"Amen," Maxine called out, in support.

Eli rewarded her with a smile, then continued. "There was a young woman that was married to a soldier. Her husband received orders reassigning him to a new duty station. The wife was a schoolteacher and didn't want to leave before the school year was over. The soldier went ahead of his wife to secure housing for them. His wife moved in with her mother-in-law while she waited for the move to take place. Stay with me now. I'm going somewhere with this story."

Trying not to bore the people, Eli stepped away from the podium and paced the stage. "One day, the young lady was looking for a scoop to make snack bags. She looked in the cabinet and found a plastic teacup. She had never seen the teacup used. It was in the cabinet with the measuring cups and bowls, which seemed out of place. The young lady reasoned if she used the cup, it wouldn't be missed because it was just sitting there. Instead of just taking up space, she figured the cup would be useful for her. She took the cup, used it, and held on to the cup instead of returning it."

"Later that week, her mother-in-law casually asked, 'Have you seen my little brown teacup?' The young lady said, 'Oh yes, I have it. I saw it in the back of the cabinet, so I didn't think anyone used it.' 'Oh,' the mother replied, 'I use it all the time. You just haven't seen me use it.' Turns out, the teacup was a family heirloom. The mother told her the history of the cup. The young woman realized what she thought was an insignificant, out-of-place cup was in fact a priceless treasure.

"Many of you are that teacup. You may appear to some as if you're out of place. You seem as if you're just sitting, being of no use. People have approached you and used you for their benefit. When they're done, they push you aside until they are ready to use you again. I'm here to tell you today. It doesn't matter who looked at you and deemed you insignificant. God has called you His treasure. You are priceless. You see, the mother-in-law told the young woman the teacup was once part of a set her father had purchased for her mother many years ago. Throughout the years, each piece of the set was broken or lost until the teacup was the only piece that remained. There may have been people attached to you. People you thought would be there for you. Those that made you promises, but one by one they fell off and disappeared from your life. You may have found yourself standing alone.

"I'm here today to tell you, God said He will never leave you. He will never forsake you. You're never alone. It doesn't matter how long the wait may seem, what God has promised you will happen. Be still, child of God, for your Father knows the plan He has for your life. Rejoice, knowing God has not forgotten you. You are a treasure."

Eli prayed for the parishioners and returned to his seat. Maxine dabbed at her eyes and returned the handkerchief to her purse. She touched her fingers to her lips before extending her hand towards Eli. With a slight nod, he acknowledged the gesture. Maxine's actions led Eli to believe his sermon had ministered to her the same as he prayed it would to everyone present. Eli was confident he was making the right decision, making her his wife.

Twenty-Six

"I ENJOYED YOUR SERMON," MAXINE SAID, HOLDING ON to Eli's arm as they walked to his vehicle. "I didn't know you could preach like that. When you didn't open your Bible, talking about you were going to tell a story, the people were giving you all kinds of side eyes. You won them over in the end."

"To God be the glory. Any time I have the opportunity to share the love of God with others, I feel elated."

"The church was packed."

"I suppose it was. I don't pay attention to the number of people in attendance. Whether there is a room full, or one person. It doesn't make a difference. I enjoy ministering."

"Be for real. With all those people, you know they collected a bunch of money. While you're trying to be all deep, I'm keeping it real."

"I'm sure a church of this magnitude has a lot of expenses."

"That may be true, but the pastor's wife was dripping in diamonds. The sister was wearing a diamond Rolex, and it wasn't fake. I would know. Not all the money they collect is used to pay bills at the church. I'm sure Pastor Youngblood is getting a cut. I know you saw that metallic gold Mercedes-Benz Maybach parked in the spot marked Pastor."

Eli opened the car door and waited for Maxine to get inside. She winked at him and pulled the seatbelt across her chest. Once he joined her inside, she continued to press him.

"Sweetheart", he said, "you can't always go by what you see. We don't know the source of his wealth. I'm sure you realize, just because someone has expensive things doesn't mean they are wealthy. Likewise, because someone isn't flashy or appears to have expensive things doesn't mean they are broke."

"Yeah, okay. I hear what you're saying, but I know what I saw." Maxine crossed her arms and looked over at Eli. She listened as he hummed the tune of a song she didn't recognize. "Eli," she called out to him. "Why aren't you a pastor? You clearly have a gift of speaking. When you were up there telling your story, the people were captivated. I don't know what it is, but you have this thing where people seem to be drawn to you. I've noticed it before. When we go out anywhere, people hang on your every word. At first, I thought nothing of it, until today. Now I know what it is. You're supposed to be a pastor."

"I'm sure I will be one day. Whenever the Lord says so." Eli reached over and caressed her cheek with the back of his finger. "I don't want to get ahead of God."

Maxine needed to get Eli on board for her plan to work. She needed to convince him to become a pastor sooner rather than later. Seeing Pastor Youngblood's wife sitting pretty at church with her Versace silk midi shirt dress, Virtus pumps and Birkin bag reminded Maxine of what she wanted. Eli still hadn't revealed the extent of his wealth, but she knew enough to know he was loaded. Being a rich man's wife wasn't enough for Maxine, she wanted it all. Wealth and prestige.

"I'm famished. What do you say we grab a bite to eat?" Eli asked.

"Sure. There's a place I've been wanting to try called Abigail's. It's an upscale soul food restaurant. They serve a peach cobbler pound cake I've heard is phenomenal." Maxine gave Eli directions to the restaurant and closed her eyes.

Abigail's was a restaurant Jonathan was adamant they could never go to. After repeated requests, he'd finally revealed it was his wife's favorite restaurant. Maxine couldn't believe she'd let Jonathan control her so much. She was so set on being the good mistress. She'd even refused an invitation from Rashida to have dinner at Abigail's. Going with Eli would be a virtual slap in Jonathan's face.

Light rain tapped against the vehicle, causing Maxine to open her eyes. "Oh no, I cannot get my hair wet."

"I have an umbrella in the back seat. I'll let you out in front of the restaurant and park the car. You get us a table and I'll meet you inside."

"Thank you, Eli. You're so good to me."

"I try my best."

Eli pulled up to the restaurant and retrieved the umbrella from the back seat. He got out and moved quickly to Maxine's side. He escorted her to the door and returned to his vehicle.

Maxine stepped inside the restaurant and looked around. The décor was beautiful. She walked over to the host stand and requested a table for two. Rather than giving the host Eli's description to join her at the table, she waited for him to come inside. Maxine admired a large tank filled with tropical fish as she waited for Eli. Suddenly, she felt fingernails dig into her skin as a firm grip tightened around her arm. She turned and found Jonathan towering over her.

"What are you doing here?" he barked. "I told you never to

come here. Are you stalking me? This isn't a game you want to play. I will crush you like a bug." Jonathan tightened his grip on Maxine's arm. "If my wife had seen you, I would've taken you outside and snatched you up."

"Man, what do you think you're doing? Get your hands off my fiancé."

Maxine and Jonathan turned and found Eli standing behind them. Maxine snatched her arm out of Jonathan's grip.

"Fiancé?" Jonathan chuckled. He looked at Maxine's hand and flared his nostrils.

"Yeah, that's right, fiancé." Eli stepped closer to Jonathan. "Now, I suggest you walk away. Otherwise, this won't end well for either of us."

"This isn't over, Maxine," Jonathan spat and walked across the restaurant to his table.

Eli pulled Maxine into his arms. "What was that about? Who's that guy?" His chest fiercely rose and fell.

Maxine could hear Eli's heart pounding against his chest. "He's my old boss. Can we please get out of here?"

"Yeah. Let's go." Eli led Maxine out of the restaurant and ushered her to the vehicle.

The adrenaline rush had dissipated. Maxine was shaking and crying. Without pretense, she spoke. "When I lost my job, it was because they accused me of omitting some important information from a legal brief, costing the firm millions. I told them it wasn't true, but they didn't believe me. I guess he still thinks it's true. He's the founding partner."

"The devil is always busy. I just preached and now this. When I came in and saw his hand on your arm, I almost knocked him out right then and there. It took all the God I have in me to keep from laying him out. I should have him arrested for assault. There were enough witnesses to collaborate our statement to the police."

With shaky hands, Maxine swatted away the tears that poured from her eyes. "I want to go home. I've never been so humiliated." She rubbed her arm, trying to soothe the pain. Jonathan had taken things to another level. The minute he put his hands on her, the game changed. If a war is what Jonathan Freeman wanted, a war is what he would get.

Twenty-Seven

MAXINE PULLED UP IN FRONT OF RASHIDA'S HOUSE AND blew her horn. She drummed her fingers on the steering wheel and waited for her friend to come outside.

"Hey, girl," Rashida squawked. She sashayed out to the car and jumped inside. "What's popping?" Rashida tapped Maxine on the arm.

"Ow, Rashi," Maxine winced and grabbed her arm.

"Girl, what's wrong with you?" Rashida asked, her face etched with confusion.

Maxine removed her arm from her sweater and showed Rashida the bruise.

"What the... Maxine? What happened to your arm? Don't tell me dude been over there whooping on you. I'm calling my brother. We'll handle this right now. I don't care how much money the brother has, he catching these hands today." Rashida pulled her phone from her pocket.

"Wait, Rashi. Eli is not beating on me. Jonathan did this."

"Jonathan? How? Wait a minute. Are you still seeing him?"

Maxine recounted the events of the previous day to her best friend. Her arm throbbed, causing tears to form from the pain.

"I knew dude was crazy. I told you he wasn't wrapped too tight. The question is, what do you want to do about it?"

"I need to get him back. I'm even willing to drop a couple thousand to get it done. Do you know anybody who's pregnant? She needs to be cute, smart, and showing. I'm going to give her intimate details about Jonathan that only someone sleeping with him would know. Since he wants to play games, it's time to pay Wifey a visit. Jonathan won't know what hit him. When he put his hands on me, he went way too far."

Rashida turned to Maxine. Her mouth open in surprise. "You're paying two Gs. Dang, girl. I got you though. I know the perfect girl. She kinda favors you, which is good. Remember that time his wife came to your job and accused you of having an affair with him? Based on your looks and that chick I saw him with at the club, he clearly has a type. When his wife sees my girl's belly, she is going to straight up lose it."

"I know, right. Jonathan messed with the wrong one. There is no way I'm letting this go. Mark my words, he is going to pay. I was trying to have a nice lunch date with Eli. Instead, I got embarrassed, and a bruised up arm."

"Speaking of Eli. Let me see your ring."

Maxine extended her hand to Rashida and wiggled her fingers.

"Oh, my God. This ring is gorgeous. Seeing it on FaceTime didn't do it any justice. Eli has good taste."

"Yes, he does. He thinks I'm mad at him about yesterday because I haven't talked to him since we got back to the house. I'm not mad. I just needed some space. When I think about it, I suppose I could be upset. Another man would have gotten physical with Jonathan, but preacher man wasn't trying to go there. Had he not spoken up the way he did, we really would have a problem. I went mute because I didn't want him to keep asking questions. I couldn't have him guessing I was once involved with Jonathan."

"I don't blame you for that."

Maxine shifted in her seat. "Rashi. Let's get back to the matter at hand. Who is this girl you have in mind? Do I know her?"

"I don't think you know her. Her name is Estelle. In the neighborhood, everybody knows her as Stella." Rashida pulled her phone from her pocket and opened her social media account. She typed Estelle Dame into the search bar. Once she had the profile pulled up, she scrolled through Estelle's pictures and showed them to Maxine.

Maxine took the phone from Rashida and zoomed in on a photo of Estelle proudly displaying her baby bump. "She's cute. I mean, she's not me, but she will do."

Twenty-Eight

Dear Lord, what kind of husband will I be if I can't protect Maxine while she's my fiancé? I should have knocked that dude out. I behaved like a coward.

Eli paced the length of his office. He walked over to the window and looked out over the car lot. His sales staff was busy interacting with customers, but he wouldn't allow himself to appreciate the moment. A loud pop echoed throughout the office as Eli's fist made contact with his open palm.

Watching Maxine cry broke Eli's heart. He knew money made people do crazy things, but to assault a woman in the middle of a restaurant was too much. If he had anything to say about it, Maxine would never work for anyone again. The idea of another man having so much access to her was unnerving. Eli wouldn't hold Maxine hostage, but he would attempt to simplify life for her by insisting she not work outside the home.

There was only one way he could have a say over her actions. Eli needed to marry Maxine, with no further delay. He moved to his desk and opened his computer. He hoped he wasn't being too presumptuous. With a few taps on the keyboard and click of the mouse, his reservations were in place. Eli pulled his cell phone from his pocket and dialed Daliah. He instructed her to explore the menu at Abigail's and to duplicate every item, including the peach cobbler pound cake. Eli's plan was to have Daliah prepare dinner for him and Maxine. Since he had no way of knowing which items Maxine would choose, he told Daliah to bring it all. Eli pinned his hopes on Maxine still desiring to marry him.

Eli: Good Morning Sweetheart. I missed you at breakfast. I'm sorry about yesterday. Let me make it up to you.

Maxine: Good Morning. Please don't remind me about yesterday. I'm trying to forget it.

Eli: I want to talk to you this evening. Can you come up to the house at six for dinner?

Several minutes passed before Maxine texted back.

Maxine: Yeah, I'll be there. I'm in the middle of something right now. TTYL.

Eli stared at the phone. Maxine's responses gave him no clue of how she was feeling. Her abbreviation of talk to you later at the end of her last text let him know the conversation was over. After the icy response, he was rethinking his dinner plans. A meal based on the menu at Abigail's could trigger an adverse reaction.

The doorbell rang, catching Eli by surprise. He looked at his watch and noted the time: 5:58 pm. Daliah had already delivered the food, so he knew it wasn't her. Eli moved swiftly to the door.

Maxine stood outside with her hands folded. Shaking her head, she tossed her hair back and looked around. Eli watched her for a moment before opening the door. Once she was inside, he pulled her into a hug. Maxine pressed her shoulder against his chest, protecting her arm.

"Why didn't you come in through the side door like you normally do? The front door seems so formal."

"You said you wanted to talk and have dinner. I didn't want to be overly casual. Especially not knowing what this is about. The phrase 'I want to talk to you' carries a lot of weight."

"I didn't mean to alarm you. This is a pleasant talk, I promise." Eli stepped aside and allowed Maxine space to enter. "I hope you brought your appetite."

"Wow, Eli, this is a lot of food," Maxine glanced around the kitchen at the containers.

"I had Daliah to prepare dinner for us. I want tonight to be special. Since I planned the menu as a surprise, I wasn't sure what you would want to eat." Eli opened his arms and pointed at the spread. "Take your pick. There is certain to be something here you will enjoy."

Maxine lifted the lids and observed the dishes. "It smells amazing in here." She turned and faced Eli. "You realize there is no way we can eat all this food, don't you?"

"I know. I'll make sure what we don't eat is put to good use." Eli walked over and picked up a small pan. He removed the lid and extended the pan to Maxine. "I had this prepared just for you."

"Oh my God! Is that peach cobbler pound cake?"

"It sure is." Eli retrieved two plates from the cabinet and handed one to Maxine. "You go first, get whatever you want."

Maxine filled her plate with grilled pork tenderloin, mac and cheese, sweet potato puree, apple walnut relish, crispy fried onions, and a cornbread muffin. She took her plate and placed it on the dinner table. "This is going to kill my diet, but I'm going to eat it anyway," she said, turning her lip up into a half smile.

Eli fixed his plate, then returned to the kitchen to fill two goblets with iced tea. He took a seat across from Maxine and extended his hand to her. She placed her hand in his while Eli blessed the food. He held on to Maxine's hand a little longer than he normally would. His thumb glided across the diamond stone on her engagement ring.

"I see you got the ring sized," he acknowledged.

"Yeah, I went earlier today. I found a jeweler that could size it the same day. It wasn't easy, especially with the diamonds on the side. It cost a pretty penny, but it was worth it."

"Had I known you were having it sized today, I would have given you my credit card. I'll give you the money you spent back after dinner. Remind me and I'll write you a check."

"I sure will." Maxine stuck her fork into the macaroni and cheese and savored the bite. "This is delicious. Thank you."

"I'm glad you're enjoying it." Eli placed his fork on the table and looked into Maxine's eyes. "Maxine, I love you. I'm glad you accepted my proposal. You did so without even knowing everything about me. Omitting information about myself was not intentional, it just worked out that way. I know you're the woman God has for me."

Maxine wrinkled her forehead. "Are you proposing again? I already accepted your proposal once. We don't have to go through this again."

"No, it's nothing like that. I believe if you're going to be my wife, you need to know everything."

"Such as?" Maxine asked, taking another bite of food.

"The car dealership, for example. I'm not only the general manager, I own the dealership. My father provided me with money to get started, but I have built the dealership on my own. Financially, I'm a millionaire many times over."

Maxine dropped her fork onto her plate, causing a large

clanking sound. "Are you serious? Why are you telling me this now?"

"You've never asked me about my financial standing, which further confirms you're the woman for me. The other reason I'm telling you this now is because I don't want a long engagement. We haven't talked about what you want regarding a wedding."

"I don't want a wedding."

Eli raised his hands and waved them in thanks. He smiled at Maxine. "More confirmation. I don't know your thoughts, but I would like to elope."

"Is that wise? Don't you need to consult your legal counsel first? It's not normal for a multi-millionaire to elope without having a prenup in place."

"I already consulted with the greatest counselor. I'm not worried about a prenup. Money doesn't rule me. I can't spend my life worried about what's going to happen to my money." Eli caressed her cheek. "I make sound business decisions. This is different. I want to spend the rest of my life with you by my side. I don't need a piece of paper causing division before we ever get started."

A smile spread across Maxine's face. Her plan was working better than she expected. "If you're sure about this, I'm all for it."

Twenty-Nine

MAXINE SAT IN THE JET SETTER LOUNGE, SURROUNDED by Eli's embrace. She couldn't believe he had purchased airline tickets on a whim. Now, here she was watching the sun rise at an airport heading to Las Vegas. Before nightfall she would be Mrs. Jasper Elijah Clayton. She couldn't believe her luck. Her plan was falling into place almost too perfectly. It was as if Eli had read her playbook and was beating her to the punch every time, but to her benefit.

The time came for them to board the flight. Eli had purchased first-class tickets. Maxine was happy because she would not have flown any other way. Sitting back against the plush leather seat, Maxine adjusted the head rest so she could lay her head comfortably against the seat. She closed her eyes and thought for a moment. She was about to marry a man she didn't love. Not only did she not love him, she wasn't even attracted to him. She reasoned Eli could provide her with a posh lifestyle. Financially, she would never have to worry about a thing. Maxine struggled to decide if she was living a dream or heading for a nightmare. Things were a little too easy.

"Are you comfortable?" Eli asked, squeezing Maxine's hand.

"I'm good, just a bit tired. I was up late last night packing. Then, of course, we got up early this morning. I think I may sleep this entire flight."

"This is a nonstop flight. We should get there in just under four hours. That should give you a pretty good nap."

Stretching her legs out under the seat in front of her, Maxine reclined and adjusted once more before nodding off. Sleep evaded her. She laid still with her eyes closed, hoping Eli would think she was asleep. Her nerves were all over the place. Everything seemed too good to be true. She realized, based on his appearance, Eli probably didn't have many romantic encounters. There had to be some, although obviously he kept his wealth hidden. Despite that, Eli had a great personality. He was genuinely a nice guy. Maxine was sure at some point, some woman tried to tie him down.

She watched as Eli drifted off to sleep. Maxine was relieved to know he didn't snore. Once they landed in Las Vegas and became man and wife, she would be forced to sleep in the bed with him. Maxine figured he would also expect her to fulfill wifely duties of intimacy. She had not been lost on the way Eli looked at her. The day she wore her pajamas to his house, he took her on his yacht and proposed. The kiss he gave her left nothing to the imagination. Maxine wasn't sure how long Eli had been celibate, but she could tell he was more than ready for that to end.

The plane touched down, and Maxine was a ball of nerves. She wondered if she could go through with marrying Eli. Marriage was an enormous commitment, even with divorce being an option. Maxine knew once she signed the papers and said *I do* to Eli, there would be no turning back. She looked over at him and struggled to find a reason other than his wealth to become his wife.

The impact of the plane landing roused Eli from his sleep. He turned to Maxine and caressed her face. "You are so beautiful, sweetheart. I love you so much and I can't wait to show you every day." He grabbed her hand and pulled it to his lips, gently planting butterfly kisses.

Maxine rewarded Eli with a genuine smile. *Perhaps marrying him won't be so bad after all*, she thought. Intimate moments didn't last forever and even then, she knew she could control them. Maxine looked at her engagement ring and thought about the life she was inheriting. She deserved this. Maxine worked hard at maintaining her appearance and being successful in her own right. She earned her job with Freeman, Reynolds, and Associates based on her credentials as a paralegal, not because of the relationship she had with Jonathan Freeman. That came later.

Having excelled in everything she did, Maxine figured being a pastor's wife would be a breeze. She didn't know any pastor's wives personally, but the few times she'd attended church, all she ever saw the wives do was sit and smile. A few of them called out amen throughout the sermon. She could handle that with no problem. Pushing all doubts aside, Maxine prepared herself to become Eli's wife.

"Good morning, everyone. Welcome to Las Vegas. The local time is 9:12 am. The current temperature is 97 degrees. Thank you for flying with us. We hope to see you again soon."

Hearing the flight attendant's announcement, Maxine rolled her eyes. "Eli, it is hot as hell fire here. I hope we don't have to do much walking because I can't do this heat."

"Don't worry about it. I'll make sure you stay cool."

"I hope you're right, because I refuse to be out here in this heat. As hot as Las Vegas is, I don't know what possessed me to agree to come out here in the middle of summer. I heard it gets so hot here in the summer, the soles of people's shoes have literally melted."

"You came because you want to marry me. As for the shoes, I can't confirm or deny the allegation. I've only been here once before for a conference, but the conference was in the winter. The temperatures weren't bad then."

The couple exited the plane and made their way to baggage claim. Maxine stood at the baggage carousel and looked around. The airport was bustling with travelers. It was a melting pot of various cultures, ages, and genders. A loud squeal drew Maxine's attention to a group of women. One woman was wearing a white tank top, bridal veil, and a white sash with the words BRIDE TO BE printed in silver letters. Her travel companions wore pink tanks with royal blue sashes. Their sashes had BRIDE SQUAD printed on the front.

Observing the obvious joy on the bride's face and the excitement of her friends, Maxine quickly looked away.

"Are you okay?" Eli asked, noticing Maxine's discomfort.

"I'm fine."

"I saw you looking at those ladies with the sashes. Are you regretting not having a wedding with bridesmaids?"

"No, Eli. I said I'm fine. Please leave it alone. We came here for a purpose, that's getting married. It's just us and I'm glad. The two of us are all we need. Half of those women probably don't even like her. There is always at least one in the bunch that either doesn't like the bride or doesn't care for the groom. I'm good. I don't need that kind of drama in my life." Maxine pointed at the carousel. "There are our bags. Can you get them, please?" She winked, urging Eli to pick up the luggage.

With bags in hand, Eli extended his elbow to Maxine. "Come on. There's our driver. He'll take us to the hotel and anywhere else you'd like to go."

The driver approached the couple and took the bags from Eli.

Maxine snuggled close to Eli. "Instead of the hotel, let's go straight to the marriage license bureau. I want to get this over as soon as possible."

Thirty

"Are you sure this is what you want?" Eli asked as they stood in front of the wedding chapel. He held Maxine's hand and squeezed it gently.

"Yes, Eli. I'm sure. Now, can you please stop asking? You asked in the car before we left the airport. Then, you asked again at the marriage license bureau. Now, we're at the wedding chapel and you're asking me again. It's as if you're waiting for me to change my mind. I wouldn't have come all this way with you if I wasn't going through with the marriage. Can we please get out of this heat and go inside? Unless you've changed your mind."

"No, I haven't changed my mind. I'm sorry if I made you feel otherwise." Eli pulled the door open and allowed Maxine to enter the building first.

The chapel was beautiful. There were fresh flowers placed throughout the room. Sheer white curtains and twin pedestals topped with rose filled vases provided a backdrop for the small white podium in the center of the room. Each row of chairs had a small flower arrangement at the base.

A boutique to the left of the chapel was filled with tuxedos and dresses. A large sign that read RENT ME hung above the entrance. Bouquets of fresh and artificial flowers of various sizes and colors took up a corner of the room.

Eli placed his hand in the small of Maxine's back and guided her towards the boutique. "Would you like to rent a dress?"

"Ew, no." Maxine frowned in disgust. "I'm not putting this body in a dress that has been worn by God only knows who. What's wrong with my outfit?" Maxine asked. Extending her arms, she turned around, giving him a full view of her one shoulder jumpsuit. The asymmetrical cut of the bright yellow top continued to the bottom of the white wide-legged pant. Her white sandals featured a line of rhinestones down the front and around the ankle strap.

"You look beautiful. I want to make this day as special for you as possible." Eli pulled at the collar of his shirt. "I'm asking about you. I should have made a better selection myself. You are stunning. I packed a suit for the occasion. Since we didn't go to the hotel first, I'm here in jeans and a polo."

Eli picked up a bouquet that contained yellow roses, white calla lilies, and daisies and handed it to Maxine. "At least let me buy you a bouquet."

"If you feel you must. A bouquet won't make us any more married than if I go empty-handed. Clearly, this is what you want, so fine." Maxine accepted the bouquet from Eli.

An officiant came out to greet them. The petite woman introduced herself as Emily Pogue. She took the large envelope containing the marriage license from Maxine and guided them to the chapel. Noting Eli and Maxine had come alone, Emily pointed out her two assistants and informed the couple the assistants would serve as their witnesses.

Together, they walked to the front of the chapel. Maxine handed her bouquet to Emily's assistant. Facing one another, Eli and Maxine stood in front of the podium, holding hands. Eli stared into Maxine's eyes and smiled. He couldn't believe the beautiful woman he met by chance in a department store was about to be his wife. Inwardly, he offered a prayer of thanks to God for his bride.

"Have the two of you written your own vows, or would you like the standard vows?"

Maxine spoke before Eli could utter a word. "We just want the basics, Emily. You know the do you take this man part. Give us enough to make it legal."

"My, someone is in a hurry to marry her beau. I've performed some speedy nuptials in the past. After all, this is Las Vegas. Have no fear. I'll give you exactly what you want."

"Thank you." Maxine returned her attention to Eli.

A smile filled Eli's face. Maxine speeding the ceremony along didn't bother him one bit. The sooner she became his wife, the better.

Emily cleared her throat and smiled at the couple. "Dearly beloved, we're gathered here today before God and these witnesses to join Maxine Miller and Jasper Elijah Clayton together in holy matrimony. Jasper, do you take Maxine to be your wedded wife?"

"I do," Eli answered, adding more bass to his voice than necessary.

Nodding, Emily continued, "Do you, Maxine, take Jasper to be your wedded husband?"

"Yes, I do," Maxine replied, never taking her eyes off Eli.

"Do you have rings you would like to exchange?"

Shaking his head, Eli exhaled in frustration. "I didn't think about the rings."

"It's okay, we can go by the jewelers when we leave here." Maxine tightened her grip on his hands.

"In that case, I suppose the only thing left for me to say is, I now pronounce you husband and wife. You may kiss if you desire."

Maxine stepped close to Eli, stood on her toes, and gave him a quick peck on the lips. Eli pulled her closer into his arms and inhaled her essence.

"You're mine now," Eli declared.

Thirty-One

MAXINE STOOD IN THE WINDOW OF THEIR HOTEL SUITE and looked out at the fountains. Using her right hand, she twirled her wedding set around her finger. She couldn't believe she had done it. She married a preacher, who also happened to be a millionaire. Maxine expected to be excited or angry, anything but the numbness she was experiencing. She wasn't sure how she was supposed to feel.

Turning away from the window, she looked around the suite. When they checked in, she couldn't hide her confusion. Eli had reserved the presidential suite. The suite included two king sized bedrooms. Rather than choosing which bedroom to occupy, she followed Eli. Noticeable shock registered on her face when he took her luggage into one bedroom before placing his luggage in the other bedroom.

"What's going on, Eli? What are you doing?" Maxine asked, frustration clear in her tone.

Eli faced her and placed his hands on her shoulders. "I imagine you were expecting us to share a bed tonight. I can hardly wait for us to solidify our marriage covenant, but I don't want it to be rushed. Coming together with you in a place that has mobile billboards advertising female companionship is not my idea of romance. You have your room, and I have mine. Should you decide you want a cuddle buddy, my door will be open. If not, it's okay. We have the rest of our lives together. There's no need to rush." Eli kissed her and left the bedroom.

Maxine slid down onto the sofa and reflected on Eli's words. The more she was around him, the more he proved he wasn't the average guy. She wasn't attracted to him, but he was growing on her. She couldn't ignore his kindness. Maxine didn't know what life would be like for them once they returned to Chicago. She even looked forward to being married.

Living on Eli's property for the past month gave them each companionship. Maxine genuinely enjoyed their meals together and movie nights. She couldn't see herself calling him husband, but she could call him a friend. The problem was, Maxine wasn't sure how long that would be enough for him.

The phone beeped. Maxine viewed the display and read the incoming text from Rashida. The decision to get married came so suddenly, Maxine didn't think to reach out to her best friend.

Rashida: It's done! Can you come by my house?

Maxine: I'm out of town. I won't be back for a couple days.

Rashida: Out of town! What are you doing out of town? Where are you?

Maxine: Eli and I are in Las Vegas.

Rashida: I know you're not in Vegas with the way you talked about me when I said I was going a while back. What are you doing in Vegas?

Maxine could tell Rashida was frustrated by the wording of her last message. If she told Rashida she and Eli had eloped, she knew her friend would stop talking to her. She couldn't let that happen, especially since she wanted to get the details of Estelle's interaction with Jonathan's wife. Maxine was careful with her reply.

Maxine: It's a long story.

Rashida: Make it short.

Rashida included an angry face emoji with her message.

Maxine: Eli had to come out here to take care of some business. He asked me to come along and I said yes.

Maxine snapped pictures of the suite, showing there were two bedrooms to collaborate with her story.

Rashida: Aww, I was about to say you better not have gone out there and got married and not said anything to me.

Maxine: Girl, please, you know better than that.

Rashida: Can you talk because it's too much to type? I'm getting tired of all this texting. Matter of fact, how about you FaceTime me instead?

Maxine: Give me a few minutes to make sure Eli is not ear hustling and I'll FaceTime you.

Rashida: Okay, bet.

Maxine ended her text exchange and went to Eli's bedroom. She tapped lightly on the door and listened for his response.

"Come on in, sweetheart." Eli sat on the edge of the bed with the television remote in his hand. "I thought you were in there resting. I've just been in here watching TV, didn't want to bother you."

"I'm going to rest for a little while. I also need to check in with my girl, Rashida." She looked at the television and noticed a baseball game on the screen. The game was going into the fifth inning. "Go ahead and finish your game. After the game, and my nap, we can grab a bite to eat. This hotel has a lot of exquisite restaurants."

"That sounds like a plan. Enjoy your nap." Eli turned and directed his attention back to the television.

Maxine padded across the suite to her bedroom and turned on the television. She hoped the sound from the television would drown out her conversation with Rashida.

Thirty-Two

MAXINE DROPPED INTO A CHAIR NEXT TO THE WINDOW, pulled up Rashida's contact information, and pressed the button for a video call. She tapped her foot in anticipation as she waited for Rashida to answer. Knowing Rashida, she would be full of questions.

Moments later, Rashida's image came into view. Rashida pasted on a huge grin. "Hey, girl. What's going on?"

"Nothing, just chilling," Maxine replied, holding the phone close to her face.

"You look like you're up to something. You better not be lying about getting married. I swear I will hurt you." Rashida tightened her eyes to a squint. "Why do you have the phone so close to your face? Back up. If you're really in a room by yourself, I want to see."

Maxine pressed the button to switch the camera from front facing to rear. She scanned the room, showing Rashida every inch. Next, she pointed the camera outside, revealing the view. Switching the camera back to the front, Maxine propped the phone up on the night table, using the view of the fountains as her background.

"I would show you Eli's room, but he thinks I'm in here taking a nap. Now stop stalling and tell me what happened with Estelle."

"I hope you're ready, because this is going to be good. Where should I start?" Rashida placed her index finger against her right temple as if she was thinking. "Okay, I got it. You know me, I'm not giving out any money until I know a job is complete. I wasn't taking any chances, so I drove Stella over to Jonathan's house. They live in a gated community, which meant I had to be creative. Girl, I had my cousin create a fake shopping app screen for my phone showing a delivery going to Jonathan's neighbor's address. I was hoping the security guard at the gate didn't call the homeowner to verify. We lucked out on that one."

"Dang. I'm impressed."

Turning her lip up, Rashida continued. "You're going to get enough of underestimating me. Anyway, when we got to the house, I dropped Stella off and parked a couple houses away. She called my phone before she made it to the door so that I could listen in on the conversation with Jonathan's wife. When wifey opened the door and saw Stella standing there with her big ole belly, she was like, 'May I help you?' talking to Stella like she was a charity case."

Maxine adjusted in her seat. Rashida was animated as she told the story, rolling her neck and changing her voice to simulate the conversation between Stella and Jonathan's wife. Maxine felt like she was there while the events unfolded.

"Then what happened?"

"Stella acted like she was offended by Wifey's reaction. She said to his wife, 'you can't help me, but Jonathan can. Is he here?' Girl, Wifey was too upset. She was like, 'I beg your pardon, what is this about?' Stella told her, 'This is about his baby, that's what.'

Stella says she turned apple red. Wifey was like, 'what baby?' Stella patted her stomach and said, 'this baby'."

"Ooh, wee, this is getting good," Maxine squealed, clapping her hands.

"I know, right. So then Wifey was like, 'I don't believe you.' Stella told her, 'You don't have to believe me, but I bet you'll believe those Tom Ford boxers he likes to wear.' Wifey wasn't falling for that. She had the nerve to tell Stella for all she knew Stella could be a salesclerk at the store where he shops, or a machine operator at the dry cleaners. Stella told her, 'I guess that green kidney bean shaped birthmark on his right butt cheek won't convince you either. Maybe you'll believe me when I describe the scar he got on his chest when he and his brother were playing in the kitchen when they were little. His brother hit the handle on a pot on the stove, causing hot grease to splash. Jonathan got hit below his clavicle.'"

Maxine placed her hand over her mouth. "Ooh, wee."

"Wifey was like, 'you stay right here'. She pulled her phone out and called Jonathan. The minute he answered the phone, his wife lit into him. She was screaming and crying. Stella said she almost felt bad for the woman, then she thought about how much she was getting paid and got over it."

"What did Jonathan say?" Maxine asked. Curiosity was eating her up.

"He told his wife he didn't know anyone name Stella. That's the name she used, by the way. So then, his wife started telling him all the personal details about him Stella told her. He started yelling and cursing. I could hear him word for word. After that, Stella turned to walk away and told Wifey to let Jonathan know she and the baby will be waiting. I swear she sounded like Sophia in *The Color Purple*. His wife slammed the front door. I picked Stella up, and we left. I'm surprised you haven't heard from him yet. Jonathan is a smart man. I'm sure he'll figure out you set the whole thing up. Even if he does, it won't matter because he still has to explain how Stella knew such intimate details."

Maxine snapped her fingers. "He probably tried to call, but he wouldn't have gotten through. I have his phone numbers blocked. Now that I think of it, I remember getting a call from an unknown number earlier today. I ignored it. It was probably him."

"I wouldn't put it past him," Rashida agreed.

"Jonathan is going to learn to leave me alone. When I cut somebody, I cut deep. He better stop playing with me."

"I'm scared of you," Rashida replied, bursting into a fit of laughter.

Thirty-Three

"IT FEELS SO GOOD TO BE HOME," MAXINE DECLARED, exiting Eli's vehicle. She stepped towards the guesthouse but was halted by Eli's hand on her shoulder. He extended a set of keys to her. "The queen of this castle shall live in the castle."

Snatching the keys from Eli's hand, Maxine laughed. "You are so corny, but I like it."

"I know that was a bit on the corny side, but what can I say? I couldn't think of anything else." He squeezed her chin between his thumb and forefinger. "From the time we left the wedding chapel, I've looked forward to bringing my beautiful wife home."

Eli unlocked the door and pushed it open. Reaching down, he swept Maxine off her feet. Eli held her in his arms and stepped across the threshold. "Welcome home, Mrs. Clayton," he said with a quick peck on her lips.

"Aww, you're so sweet. Will you please put me down now? After the long drive from the airport, I need to use the facilities."

"Of course," Eli replied. He placed her legs down first, allowing her to steady herself before he released her.

Maxine made her way to the powder room and pulled her

phone from her pocket. The notifications showed six missed calls from a number Maxine didn't recognize. She suspected the calls were from Jonathan, but since the caller didn't leave any voicemails, she couldn't say for sure.

Maxine sent a text message to the phone number displayed on her screen.

Maxine: Who is this and why do you keep calling me?

A response came almost immediately.

Jonathan: You know exactly who this is, Maxine. Stop playing around and answer the phone.

Maxine grew nervous. She knew Jonathan was a powerful man and capable of almost anything. Perhaps she had gone too far in her plot for revenge. Maxine wrestled with her thoughts when the phone rang, startling her. The device danced in her hand as she struggled to keep from dropping it. Taking a deep breath, she answered the call before it went to voicemail.

"Hello," she answered, struggling to sound confident.

"What you did was dirty, sending a pregnant girl to my house. I'm still trying to convince my wife I don't have a baby on the way."

Jonathan's calm demeanor confused Maxine. It was scary. Jonathan was coming across a bit too calm for Maxine's taste. She was prepared for yelling and even cursing. At least then she would have known how to react. She listened in silence, waiting for the Jonathan she knew to reveal himself.

"I have to hand it to you. It was a brilliant plan. My wife will be upset for quite a while. Probably until no baby surfaces. In the meantime, I'll keep trying to convince her a disgruntled former employee from one of my other businesses set everything up."

"Jonathan, what do you want?" Maxine asked with all sincerity. She was tired of his rambling and quite ready for the conversation to end.

"I want to call a truce. I'll admit I was wrong for grabbing your arm at the restaurant. You must understand, I was there with my wife and daughter. When I looked up and saw you at the front of the restaurant, I thought you were coming to cause trouble. I told my wife I had to use the restroom, so she didn't question me leaving the table. Neither my wife nor daughter saw you, nor our exchange. Why were you there?" Jonathan asked, his tone still even.

"Eli and I were there for lunch. You know I've always wanted to go there. When you and I were together, you forbade me because it was your wife's favorite restaurant. I had no way of knowing you would be there. I was done with you after our conversation in the elevator when you had me fired. Locking me out of the condo and putting my belongings in a storage unit in the hood was the last straw. I want nothing else to do with you."

"Again, I'll admit, the way I handled things was wrong. You have to understand, knowing you were seeing another man was too much. Especially with you being my woman. We were together for a long time. We may have been through a lot, but no matter what, you knew I loved you. Who am I kidding? I still love you. I miss you, Maxine."

Leaning against the wall, Maxine fought back tears. This was the Jonathan she knew and loved. The man who made sure she had whatever her heart desired. Her passionate lover. "I miss you too," she admitted, barely above a whisper.

Jonathan played on Maxine's vulnerability. "Baby let's stop this foolishness. Can we work things out?"

A light tap came on the powder room door. "Sweetheart, are you alright in there?" Eli asked. "Do you need anything?"

"I'm fine," Maxine called out, trying to sound as normal as possible.

"Who was that?" Jonathan questioned, his tone indignant.

"A lot has changed in my life, Jonathan. That was Eli," Maxine paused, allowing the silence to linger. "My husband."

The phone line went dead.

Maxine left the powder room and found Eli in the kitchen. He looked up and found her walking toward him. "Hey there, I'm grabbing a snack. Would you like a sandwich or something?"

"No, I'm fine, thank you. I'm a little tired. Perhaps it's a touch of jet lag. I prefer to lie down for a bit, if that's okay. Will you show me where I'll be sleeping?"

Eli crossed the room and stood in front of Maxine. He took her hands in his and kissed them. "I was hoping you would be ready to join me in the master suite and share my bed. It's comfortable, and big enough for you to have space if you want."

"That's fine." Maxine was in no mood to debate. She knew at some point Eli would expect her to move into his bedroom. "I've never been upstairs. Can you show me to our bedroom?" Maxine had a mischievous glint in her eyes.

"With pleasure," Eli replied. Taking Maxine by the hand, he led her upstairs to their bedroom.

Maxine laid next to Eli, spent. Hearing Jonathan's voice as he declared his love for her, and his apologies, made her crave intimacy. Her desire to be held overshadowed the lack of attraction to Eli. The gentle, caring way Eli embraced her fulfilled her need. Maxine often wondered how she would feel when things between her and Eli turned physical. She was pleased to see she wasn't disgusted, making the idea of a life with him tolerable.

"I love you, sweetheart," Eli uttered as he drifted off to sleep with Maxine in his arms.

"I love you, Jonathan," Maxine mouthed, being careful not to allow any words to escape. She snuggled closer to Eli, imagining he was Jonathan.

Thirty-Four

"ARE YOU JUST ABOUT READY?" ELI CALLED OUT TO Maxine who was yet to emerge from her closet. They had been married for less than four weeks. Eli was eager to show off his new bride at church. Maxine always had an excuse when he previously asked her to join him for Sunday service. This time, she relented and agreed to go. Eli believed in being prompt. Maxine's lagging was threatening to make them tardy.

"Almost," Maxine yelled back. "Why don't you go downstairs and grab a bite to eat or something? Make sure it's something healthy. I'll be down in a minute."

"Please hurry, okay."

"I will. Now go, you're making me nervous. You're going to make me mess up my makeup."

"I keep telling you, you don't need that stuff. You're beautiful without it."

"If you think I'm showing up at church on your arm without makeup, you're crazy."

Eli went downstairs and heated an egg white omelet that Maxine had Daliah prepare for him beforehand. He was grateful to have a wife who cared about his health. After Maxine moved in, she had Daliah prepare healthy meals Eli could easily heat and eat, both at home and at work. Maxine's insistence on them working out together had him rolling out of bed at five o'clock every morning.

His wife's tactics were paying off. Eli had already dropped fifteen pounds. His clothes were fitting nicer, and he genuinely felt better. He found the lack of sleep in the morning didn't hinder his day. The workouts made him more energetic, preventing the mid-day lag he often felt at work around lunchtime.

Approaching Eli from behind, Maxine massaged his shoulders, drawing his attention. He turned and whistled, taking in the full view of her. The coral, form fitting, side ruffle dress boasted a modest surplice neckline accentuating her feminine assets while remaining appropriate for the occasion.

"My, my, my. Mrs. Clayton, you look so good. I don't know if I should take you to church or back upstairs."

"You're so silly," Maxine gushed, tapping him on the shoulder.

Eli took Maxine's hand and turned her around. "That color looks good on you."

"I'm glad you like it. Now let's get out of here. I know you don't want to be late."

Services had already begun when Eli escorted Maxine into the church. He walked with her to the front pew and sat her next to Fredericka Scott before taking his place on the platform next to Pastor Scott and Zachariah.

Zachariah leaned over and shook Eli's hand. "Is that her?" he asked in a whisper.

"Yeah, man, that's Maxine, my wife," Eli answered, sticking his chest out with pride.

Overhearing the conversation, Pastor Scott looked at Eli's

hand. Pointing to the wedding band, he urged, "Elder Clayton, I need to see you for a moment after service."

Eli nodded his response.

At the end of the service, Eli took Maxine by the hand and the two went to Pastor Scott's office. With a few light taps on the door, Pastor Scott invited them inside.

"Oh, Elder Clayton, I see you brought your lovely wife with you. I was hoping to speak to you alone, but this is fine," Pastor Scott acknowledged.

"I hold no secrets from my wife. We can speak freely in front of her."

"Henpecked already, I see," Pastor Scott said, laughing himself into a fit.

Maxine rolled her eyes. "Excuse me?"

"I'm just kidding, Sister Clayton. Your husband knows I meant no harm. We kid around all the time." Pastor Scott continued to speak, hindering a response from the couple. "Elder Clayton, you have been an intricate part of this ministry for quite some time. I thought you and I had a good relationship and you respected me as your pastor."

Pastor Scott folded his hands and placed them on top of his desk. "As your spiritual leader, I should have been informed prior to your nuptials. Where did you get married? Who performed the ceremony? Did you receive premarital counseling?" Pastor Scott closed his eyes as if he was disgusted. "I'm quite disappointed in you, Elder."

"With all due respect, Pastor. You may be my pastor, but you are not my God. I'm sure I don't have to remind you I'm a grown man. As for counseling, I spoke with the counselor of all counselors. Our marriage is between us and God. We don't have to answer to you or anyone else concerning our marriage. The same way I wouldn't expect you to answer to me regarding your marriage to Sister Scott."

Showing his palms, Pastor Scott nodded in Eli's direction. "I didn't mean to offend you. As a man, a married man at that, I understand your stance. As your pastor, God holds me accountable for you. It's my duty to watch out for you." He pointed at Maxine. "This wife of yours is quite beautiful. You're a blessed man, Elder Clayton. Although I didn't counsel you beforehand, know that if you or Sister Clayton need me in the future, I'm here."

"Thank you." Eli stood to leave.

"Before you go, Elder," Pastor Scott continued. "A few months back, I spoke with you about a project I wanted to get done here at the church. We've done some further research and are ready to move forward. I need to get with you soon on the details of the donation I requested for the raffle. The day is far spent. If it's okay with you, I'll call you in the morning to finalize the plans."

"Call me tomorrow," Eli answered pointedly before leading Maxine out of the pastor's office.

The parishioners had cleared out by the time Eli and Maxine exited the church. Opening the car door for Maxine, he allowed her to slide inside before joining her.

Maxine kicked off her shoes and turned to Eli. "I love these shoes, but they hurt. Is there any way I can talk you into a foot rub?" she purred.

"I believe a foot rub is in order." He pulled off the church parking lot and drove toward home. "How did you like the service today? Did you enjoy the sermon?"

"The service was alright. I don't much care for Pastor Scott's preaching style. As for his personality, he almost made me forget where I was when he was talking crazy in the office. I understand he's the pastor and all, but he is not God. If you hadn't checked him, I was going to."

"Sometimes pastors allow their position to go to their heads.

Not all pastors are like that, but there are some, especially in our community, that let what they perceive as power make them forget they are dealing with adults." Eli placed his hand on Maxine's thigh and continued. "I can tell you right now, when God allows me to step into the position of pastor, I won't be that way."

"What's stopping you? From what I've seen, you're a much better preacher than Pastor Scott. Plus, you run a very successful car dealership, which means you have superb management skills. From what I hear, church is eighty percent business. There's really not a reason for you not to become a pastor now."

Pondering her words, Eli gently squeezed her thigh. "I don't know. There isn't much hindering me. I used to say I wanted to be married before starting the church. God has answered that prayer by blessing me with you. Some members of the congregation have even told me if I ever start a church, they would join with me."

"See. There you go," Maxine said, raising her hands as if she'd spoken something brilliant. "What is this donation he was talking about?"

Eli filled Maxine in on the details of Pastor Scott's request for a vehicle donation for the church raffle.

"Ooh," Maxine squealed. "That's a great idea."

Confused, Eli removed his hand from her thigh. "You like the idea of donating a vehicle. Do you have any idea how much money that amounts to?"

"Doesn't matter. We can afford it. There's only one thing."

"What's that?"

"Instead of doing it for Pastor's Scott's church, we can implement the idea at our own church. If you're serious about becoming a pastor, I can help you make it happen. I'm pretty much home all day anyway. This will give me something productive to do." Maxine rubbed the back of his head. "After all, you said you prefer I not work outside the home. Helping organize the church will give me something to do, keeping me from boredom."

Eli pondered Maxine's words. He had prayed for a wife that would support him and help him. Here she was, pushing him towards what he believed to be his destiny. Being in leadership roles in the church and in business, Eli knew what it took to be successful. Perhaps Maxine was right. Pastor Scott had some good ideas to grow the church. Stealing his ideas would lack integrity, but if the purpose was to build the community and the church, Eli felt his actions would be justified.

"Okay, if you have time tomorrow, could you scout out a few locations for me? I want the church to be in an area where it's needed and can serve the community."

"I already know the perfect location. It was once a church, but as the congregation grew, they relocated. The building has been on the market for quite some time. I'm sure we could get a great deal."

"It looks like we're about to start a church, First Lady Clayton."

"Looks like it, Pastor Clayton."

Thirty-Five

"I CAN'T BELIEVE YOU ELOPED. YOU LIED TO ME. I ASKED you straight up when you were in Vegas if you got married and you said no. I was in Chicago doing your dirty work while you were off getting married. That's messed up." Rashida crossed her arms and stared up at Maxine.

"You didn't ask me *if* I was getting married when I was in Vegas. You said I better not *be* getting married. There's a difference." Maxine placed her arm around Rashida's shoulder to soothe her friend. "It's been two months, Rashi. When are you going to get over it?"

"When do you think?" Rashida huffed. "Don't answer that. I'll tell you. I'm going to be mad about this for a very long time. It doesn't matter how many times you invite me over to the house, or how many times we go out on Eli's yacht."

"Stop playing and let's get inside. We're already late for our appointment." Maxine turned Rashida toward the door and pushed her inside the spa.

"Hello ladies, it's great to see you again," the receptionist greeted. "We have a full day together. It looks like we have you scheduled for the five-star treatment. We'll start the day with the dermal infusion body treatments, which includes the vacuum massage followed by lunch. After lunch, you will have your facials, manicures, pedicures, and lastly, your hair styled. Because of the intensity of the dermal infusion body treatment, we'll have to separate you ladies. You'll see each other again at lunch."

A woman wearing soft pink scrubs came out and escorted Rashida to the back.

"Let me go ahead and give you my credit card now," Maxine said to the receptionist. "By the time we're done, the last thing I will want to do is pay a bill."

"Trudy, her services are on me," a male voice called from behind Maxine.

Maxine turned, eyes widening in surprise. "Jonathan, what are you doing here? How did you know I was here? Have you had someone following me?"

"I have my ways of keeping tabs on you. When we were together, you were at this spa twice a month. You're high maintenance. I figured your routine hadn't changed much." He turned to Trudy and asked her to excuse them. Jonathan pulled Maxine to a set of chairs nestled in the corner near a large potted plant. "When you said you were married, I didn't believe you. I figured the marriage had to have taken place rather quickly, so I took a stab in the dark and started with the obvious. You know I have resources. It took little effort to find out you were married in Las Vegas."

"I'm not your property, Jonathan. How dare you investigate me?"

"Baby, you're misunderstanding. The last time we spoke, you said you miss me. I've told you how much I still love you. Hearing a man in the background, and having you say he's your husband, threw me into a rage I can't explain." Jonathan grabbed Maxine's hands. He examined her wedding rings. "Hmm, cute."

Jonathan stood and pulled Maxine up with him. "Let's get out of here. We can go someplace where we can talk in private. I'm paying for your spa service, you won't lose any money. You're not scheduled to see your friend again until lunchtime. That gives us at least two hours. I'll get a room. We can talk there without interruption."

Inhaling the fragrance of his cologne, Maxine closed her eyes. She couldn't believe he was wearing Azēl, the cologne she purchased for him from a boutique perfumer. It was hard enough putting Jonathan out of her mind when she didn't see or talk to him. Having him in her presence made him almost impossible to resist.

"I can't, Jonathan, it's not right. I'm a married woman."

"And. What's that supposed to mean? I'm a married man. I want to talk to you, baby. That's all." Jonathan rubbed the back of Maxine's hands with his thumbs. "What do you say?"

"Just talk?" Maxine questioned.

"Just talk. You have my word," Jonathan replied.

"I have to be back by lunch. No exceptions. If I'm not here to meet Rashida, it won't be good."

"You'll be back. Now stop stalling. Let's go."

Maxine went to the reception desk and beckoned for Trudy. "Something has come up. I need to step away for a moment. I'll be back in time to have lunch with my friend."

Gathering her belongings, Maxine went into the bathroom with tear filled eyes. She couldn't believe she had been so weak. After all the hurt and even physical pain Jonathan caused her, she allowed herself to be back in his arms. Maxine didn't expect to feel bad for cheating on Eli, but she did. She was no stranger to being involved with married men, but she vowed when she got married she'd be faithful.

Eli was a good husband. Everything Maxine asked of him, he did. Adhering to her strict diet and exercise routine, he'd lost close to forty pounds. Whatever her heart desired, Eli made sure she had it. They had even started the process of obtaining a charter for their church. Here she was, a pastor's wife, spending time in the hotel room of another man.

Riddled with guilt, Maxine freshened up and returned to the spa. She changed into a white terry cloth robe and slippers and went to the patio to wait for Rashida.

"Ooh, girl, that treatment was no joke." Rashida plopped down in the chair next to Maxine and grabbed a large strawberry from the bowl of fresh fruit on the table between them. "I'm so relaxed my legs feel like noodles. How was your treatment?"

"It was good. I've been getting these on the regular. It's not as exciting as it was in the beginning. I'm looking forward to getting my hair styled."

Rashida looked at Maxine's disheveled tresses and frowned. "Your technician must not have known what she was doing. She jacked your hair up during the scalp massage."

"Tell me about it."

The food was delivered, offering Maxine a reprieve from her conversation with Rashida. Guilt ate away at Maxine like a flesh eating disease. She felt bile rise in her throat. She closed her eyes and took a deep breath.

"Maxine, what's up with you? You are acting totally different than you did before we left the reception area. Did something happen?" Rashida dropped her fork. "Girl, did somebody take advantage of you? You can tell me. I swear we will sue this place. You'll be owning this spa."

"No, Rashida. I'm good. I just have a lot on my mind."

"Like what? I mean, the whole point of a spa day is so you can relax. You went from relaxed to tense. Don't play me like a fool. I know you better than anybody else, Maxine. Tell me what's going on?"

"It's nothing for you to be concerned about. Let's enjoy the rest of our day. We came here to have a good time. I'm not about to let unnecessary drama ruin it. I'm probably overthinking things."

Maxine wanted to share her indiscretions with her best friend, but she couldn't bring herself to verbalize her actions. Maxine was more concerned about facing Eli than she was about explaining things to Rashida.

Thirty-Six

MAXINE ARRIVED HOME, PARKED HER CAR, AND QUIETLY entered the house. She didn't expect Eli home for at least an hour. All she wanted to do was go upstairs, slide into the bathtub, and soak. She shared many intimate moments with Jonathan over the past couple of years. Despite the circumstances surrounding their relationship, being with Jonathan never made her feel dirty, until now.

The buzz of her cell phone pulled Maxine back to the present. She pulled the device from her purse and looked at the display. The unknown number Jonathan previously called from displayed on the screen. She immediately sent the call to voicemail.

Maxine paced her bedroom, feeling like a crazy person. "Let's go somewhere and talk, he said. Nothing will happen, he said. Ugh, how could I be so stupid?" She repeatedly bashed herself until her voice became hoarse.

Stripping her clothes off, Maxine decided a shower was better. She hoped the water would wash her guilt away. Steam from the hot water filled the bathroom, fogging up the mirror and windows. Maxine stood in the water and scrubbed her body until her skin was red from the harsh treatment.

Unable to stand the pain any longer, she exited the shower, wrapped herself in a plush robe and laid across the bed. Tears flowed until her eyes were burning and swollen. She cried herself to sleep.

"Sweetheart, are you okay?" Eli asked, awakening Maxine.

"Huh?" Maxine opened her eyes and struggled to focus on her husband.

"Are you feeling alright? The door was unlocked when I got home. I was concerned, so I ran up here to check on you and found your clothes strewn all over the bedroom. You've never done that. Did something happen? Are you ill?" Eli touched Maxine's forehead, checking for fever.

Maxine sat up in the bed. "Really? I didn't realize I left the door unlocked. I came home, took a shower, and fell asleep. I'm sorry about the clothes. This has been a crazy day."

"I thought you were going to the spa with your friend."

"Something came up," Maxine snapped.

"Whoa, where did that tone come from?"

"I'm stressed, Eli. I've been working so hard to get this church together. Filing paperwork, taking meetings with everyone from building contractors to potential staff members. I'm overwhelmed. I didn't realize starting a church would be this much work. You know what, I almost regret suggesting we start a church."

"You have worked hard. I appreciate all you've done. Before we have our official launch, I'm taking you on a trip. Wherever your heart desires, we can go. Better yet, you can make it a girl's trip. I'll pay for you, your best friend, and whoever else you want to take with you."

"Are you serious?" Maxine looked at Eli with hopeful eyes.

"Of course, I'm serious. I'll never lie to you."

Eli's words caused an even greater guilt to overtake Maxine. She allowed her tears to flow, knowing he would think they resulted from his offer.

"I was so concerned about you, I almost forgot. I have some good news." Eli pulled an envelope with documents from his bag. "The charter for the church came today. We're official. What a Mighty God Cathedral is a registered religious institution in the State of Illinois. How does it feel, First Lady Clayton?"

"Congratulations, Pastor Clayton. All we need now is a building."

"Thus, part two of my good news. The realtor called this morning. They have moved the closing date on the property up to the first of next week. We can have our first service in as little as six weeks."

Maxine wrapped her arms around Eli and gave him a tight squeeze. "This is wonderful. We are going to make such an impact in this city. Our church will be bursting at the seams. Wait and see. This time next year, What a Mighty God Cathedral will be known not only in Chicago, but people will be talking about us all over the nation. When we institute the online church, we can stream the services worldwide. The more people we expose to the ministry through our outreach programs, the more they will show their support financially."

Eli kissed Maxine on the forehead. "It's not about the money for me. I want to impact lives."

"And you will. Financial support will play a major role in that. All the programs we want to implement require money to function. I'm aware you have plenty of your own money, but we are not financing this church from our pockets. If you listen to me, every program we talked about, we'll be able to make happen. The community center, no cost daycare, housing assistance."

"I trust you. Eventually, we'll be able to get it all done."

"You say that like you don't believe me. Do you know what

I'm capable of?" Maxine grabbed Eli's chin and turned his face to hers. "You have no clue who you married, do you?"

"Yes. I do. Why do you think I married you?"

"You tell me all the time. You married me because I'm beautiful, but you need to know I'm more than a pretty face. I'm a very intelligent woman. The sooner you realize it, the better off we'll be."

"Where is all this coming from? We went from celebrating to I don't know what. Is there something going on I should know about?"

"No, I'm just tired of being underestimated. I've worked hard my entire life. People always want my help to build their projects. After I've fulfilled their purposes, I seem to become disposable."

"You seem to be in a fight, but sweetheart, your fight is not with me. You already said you had a hard day. I love you. I will not add to whatever has you upset. But, please hear my heart when I tell you, I'm also not going to be your punching bag."

Thirty-Seven

"Rashi, I need a big favor." Maxine spoke in a quick, desperate tone.

"What's up, Maxine. Why you sound all panicked?" Rashida scanned the sales rack. Since assisting Maxine with getting revenge on Jonathan, shopping sprees on Maxine's dime had become common.

She turned Rashida by her shoulder, gaining her full attention. "Can you cover for me? I'm going away for a few days and if asked, I need you to say I was with you. I promise I'll make it worth your while. Whatever you want, it's yours."

"Hold up. What do you have going on that you need a cover, First Lady Maxine?"

"Really. You're going to bring that up."

"You asked for the role, girlfriend. It was all a part of your grand scheme. I guess now you're implementing the other part where you'll have another man fulfill your physical needs."

Maxine frowned. "What's wrong with you? Why are you tripping?"

"I'm not tripping. I told you from the beginning, I don't

play with God. Plus, Eli is a cool dude. I like him, and you know the man is crazy about you. He has lost close to fifty pounds for you. Not to mention his regular visits to the dermatologist. I don't know how you did it, but you got a good man."

"Girl, nobody is playing with God. You don't know where I'm going or what I'll be doing, and you know what? I'm not going to tell you. Then you won't have to worry about falling off your high horse." Maxine chose not to address the comment about Eli.

"Whatever. You can't get mad at me for not wanting to be a part of you cheating on your husband."

"What makes you think I'm cheating on Eli?"

"Be for real. I've known you for more years than I can remember. We've done some dirt together. You're my friend and I love you. I'm just not about the nonsense. Alvin and I are getting closer. For the first time in my life, I think I would like to be married. I have committed to joining the church you and Eli established. I don't want to know the woman everyone is looking up to ain't right."

Showing her palms, Maxine stepped back. "Forget I asked. It's not even that deep."

Rashida turned back to the clothing rack. "You can say forget it all you want. At the end of the day, whether you choose to accept it or not, I know you heard me. By the way, while we're changing subjects, when was the last time you talked to, or better yet, seen your mother? I saw her coming out of Little Company of Mary. We talked for a good ten minutes. I noticed she didn't mention your marriage, so I didn't bring it up either. Does she know you got married?"

Maxine smacked her lips. "If she does, it's not because I told her. You know my mother and I haven't been on the best terms in a long time."

Rolling her eyes, Rashida said, "Did you hear where I said I saw her?"

"Yeah, Little Company of Mary, the hospital. What about it? Why were you there?"

"Never mind about me. Your mother was the one wearing the hospital bracelet. Girl, go check on your mother."

The ladies continued shopping as if no tension had passed between them. Maxine was disappointed at Rashida's reaction. She was counting on her to be her alibi. More than anything, she was surprised. Maxine and Rashida had been friends for a long time. They always had each other's backs. Now it appeared since Rashida was dating a preacher, she was becoming self-righteous.

Maxine didn't have time to forge another friendship, nor train another ally. She would just have to be careful and keep her interactions private, even from Rashida. Hearing Rashida's reaction, Maxine was happy she didn't tell Rashida about her affair with Jonathan. An affair which, despite her initial guilt, had continued. Jonathan made a convincing argument. With both being married, neither had expectations of their interactions being more than physical. Jonathan was a skilled lover and they had history. When it came to him, Maxine allowed her physical desires to overshadow all reasoning.

For the affair to work, Maxine had to be intentional in her treatment of Eli. If she suddenly stopped being intimate with him, or treated him less than kind, he would know something was up. Maxine and Jonathan kept their rendezvous to once weekly.

The church was scheduled to launch in two weeks. Since Jonathan had an out-of-town business trip coming up, Maxine felt it would be the best time to cash in on the trip Eli promised her. She and Jonathan could spend several days together without looking over their shoulders. The thought of four days in Hawaii with the man she couldn't get enough of made her heart skip a beat.

"What do you think about this top?" Rashida asked, holding a shirt up in front of Maxine, regaining her attention.

"It's cute. You should get it." Maxine hoped Rashida hadn't noticed her mind was elsewhere. It didn't work.

"Where is your head at? You are clearly not here because this top is straight up ugly. Are you thinking about what I said about your mother?"

"Yes," Maxine lied. "I wonder what she was doing at the hospital. She must have been there for some tests. But I'm not sure what type of testing she would need. My mother has always been very healthy. If she was there for sickness or a procedure, they would have discharged her in a wheelchair. Since you didn't mention a wheelchair, I'm going to believe she was there for routine testing."

"Don't stand there trying to guess. Go see your mother. You only have one mother and when she's gone, you won't be able to get her back."

"She's been gone. My mother is the one who cut off communication because I wasn't living my life the way she thought I should. Remember? Parents trip me out. They will stop talking to you or disown you when you don't make decisions they agree with, but when you voice your opinion over something in their life, they're quick to tell you to stay out of their business."

"I know it hurt you when you and your mom had the falling out, but that's beside the point. Life is precious and tomorrow is not promised. It's time for you to forgive and move forward. As much as they don't like to admit it, parents make mistakes too."

Thirty-Eight

Eli arrived home and found Maxine sitting at the kitchen table. She took small sips from a teacup. Running her finger around the rim of the cup, she looked up at him. Eli leaned down and kissed her on the forehead.

"How are you doing, sweetheart?" Eli asked, taking a seat at the table next to her.

"I'm fine. I've been sitting here thinking."

"Is that so? You seem awful deep in thought. What's on your mind?"

"We have been to your parents' house a few times since getting together. Your mother seems to be warming up to me, but she keeps me at arm's length. It's as if she doesn't want to get too close, which is cool. I'm good. Your father has been super cool. When we first got back from Las Vegas and you told them we were married, he was a little stand-offish, but he came around. Your mother, not so much."

"Your relationship with my mother is what's bothering you?" Eli asked.

"Honestly, no. Thinking about your mother made me realize

you've never asked me about *my* mother. I recall one conversation we had when you asked if I had siblings, but other than that, you haven't asked me anything about my mother. Nor have you expressed any interest in meeting her."

"I apologize. It's easy to see how my actions, or lack thereof, could be interpreted as uncaring. I assure you, that's not the case. You told me you were raised by your grandmother. In the time we've been together, you haven't really brought your mother up. I felt it was better for me not to bring her up in case there was some tension there. I have no objections to meeting your mom." Eli caressed her cheek. "Why don't you invite her over for dinner? Let me know when. I can have Daliah prepare a formal meal for us."

"I don't know if I'm ready to go as far as us having dinner together. I need to call her. Rashida said she saw my mother coming out of the hospital. Apparently, my mother was wearing a hospital bracelet."

Eli reached over and grabbed Maxine's hand. "Is your mother okay?" Concern etched his face. Deep lines littered his features.

"I hope so, but I don't know. I've been sitting here since I got home, trying to get the courage to call her. The last time we talked, the conversation didn't go well."

"Was it after you helped her with the insurance situation?"

Maxine frowned, "Insurance situation? What insurance situation?"

"On our first date, she texted you when we were at dinner. You said it had something to do with insurance."

"Oh, yeah." Maxine took a deep breath. She'd forgotten she told Eli her mother was texting her during dinner when it had been Jonathan. How he remembered that was beyond her. Maxine noted she would have to do a better job of keeping up with any lies she told, because Eli didn't appear to forget things easily.

"You're aware of the issue, so what are you going to do about it? I know you. You're a problem solver. Look at the work you put in helping to get the church established. You've got this. I'll be right here to support you in any way I can."

Eli kissed the back of Maxine's hand and left the table.

Maxine pondered her husband's words. Perhaps, both he and Rashida were correct. It was time for her to work things out with her mother. Maxine looked at her phone laying on the table. "I might as well get this over with," she said aloud. Sliding the phone closer, Maxine went to her contacts and selected her mother's phone number.

Rose Miller answered the call with no preamble. "I had a feeling you would be calling. I suppose I have Rashida, with her big mouth, to thank."

"Hello to you too, Mama. I'm doing well. How are you?"

"Are you sassing me?" Rose snapped.

"No, Mama, I'm not. I called to see how you're doing. We haven't talked in a while. I hoped we could have a conversation."

"I see. Well, we're doing fine over here. What about you? Are you still messing around with that woman's husband?"

"Really, Mama. You're going to go straight there, huh?" Maxine exhaled between her teeth in frustration. "I didn't call you to fight. Can we please have a civil conversation? A lot has happened in my life you are not aware of. I want to share it with you. As for your question, no. I'm no longer seeing him," Maxine lied. Although she was no longer in a full-fledged relationship with Jonathan, she was still seeing him.

"Tell me, what's been going on? I'm sure I've missed a lot. You always seem to have a lot going on." Rose's tone softened. "I'm giving you a hard time, but I'm happy to hear from you. You might not think so, but I miss you. I've been thinking about you a lot lately."

Tears formed in Maxine's eyes. Hearing her mother say she

missed her was like putting salve on an open wound. She found herself opening up in ways she hadn't imagined.

"I miss you too. I no longer work at the law firm."

"Really? I thought you loved your job. What are you doing for work now?"

"I was just about to tell you." Maxine's voice rose in excitement. "I'm married."

"You're what?" Rose's tone matched her daughter's. "Oh Lord, you didn't take that woman's husband, did you? If he cheated on her with you, he'll cheat on you with somebody else."

"Mama!" Maxine exclaimed.

"I'm sorry. Go ahead."

"My husband's name is Eli Clayton. He owns a car dealership, and" Maxine paused for dramatic effect, "he's a preacher."

"A preacher. Maxine, stop playing with me." Rose didn't mask her laughter.

"I'm not playing. We've been married for three months. Our church is launching in a couple of weeks. I would love for you to be at our inaugural service. We bought the church on 55th. You know the big one that's been empty for a while."

"That big ole church on the corner of Morton?"

"Yep, you got it."

"Chile, I suppose I've missed more than I thought. Are you still living downtown in the condo?"

"No. We live in Burr Ridge. I would love for you and Pops to come out for a visit. We can have dinner and the two of you can get to know Eli."

"Eli, huh? I always knew you'd marry a rich man."

"What makes you think he's rich?" Maxine asked, chuckling.

"I know my daughter. Besides, if this man owns a car dealership, you're living in Burr Ridge, and you got a big church building, he ain't broke. This I know for sure." Rose cackled. "I suppose the part I'm most shocked by is him being a pastor.

You're my daughter and I love you, but I've never pictured you as a pastor's wife. Are you sure you're ready for such an immense responsibility?"

"I'm ready. I have a closet full of hats and handbags."

"Honey, it's more to being a first lady than hats and handbags. If you're thinking you only have to look pretty and say amen every now and then, you're in for a rude awakening."

"You and Grandmama raised me to be a strong woman. I'm not worried. Whatever comes with the position, I can handle it." Maxine redirected the conversation. "I feel like I have dominated this entire conversation. What's going on with you, Mama? Why were you at the hospital?"

"There ain't no telling what Rashida told you. I'm sure she made it sound more dramatic than it was. I was there for a routine mammogram. It's nothing for you to be alarmed about. You know your mama. I take good care of myself. I don't have time to be getting sick."

Relief swept over Maxine like a summer breeze. She was happy to know her mother was doing well. The conversation started off rocky, but she was glad she pressed on. It felt good talking to her mother. Maxine couldn't wait to have her parents over to the house for them to see how she was living. She purposely didn't mention the yacht. Maxine would rather surprise them with that bit of information in person.

After making dinner plans, Maxine ended the call. Next, she sent a text to Rashida.

> Maxine: I called my mom, we talked. Thank you for pushing me.

Thirty-Nine

"Oh my God, Eli. Everything looks so good. People are already lining up, waiting for the festivities to start. I know I gave you a hard time when you first suggested having a carnival before the church launch, but this was a great idea."

Maxine and Eli walked the church grounds, looking at the various carnival attractions. They set up five inflatable bouncy houses. There were prize tables, basketball hoop games, Skeet ball, ring toss games, a dunking booth, concession stands with hotdogs, burgers, pizza, popcorn, cotton candy, various juices and soft drinks. Artists were on hand for face painting and caricature drawings. There was even a puppet show for the smaller children.

Eli held Maxine's hand as they walked. "From the beginning, we said our church would be community centered. We will help people spiritually, physically, emotionally, and any other way we can. I want to minister to the total person, not just preach a sermon and send people on their way. I know you were upset about the cost, initially, but look around. When we show the community we care about them body, soul, and spirit, they will respond by supporting the ministry."

"Of course, they are showing up for the carnival," Maxine interjected. "People like free stuff. I'll admit, I was upset in the beginning, especially when you wanted to pay for the carnival all by yourself. But I got on board, made a few phone calls, and got us some corporate sponsorships. It cut our costs tremendously."

"Yes, it did. That's one of the many reasons I love you. You're gifted in so many areas, always thinking on your feet. You have added so much to me and the ministry. There's no way I could have done this without you."

"I'm glad you realize it," Maxine teased. She enjoyed the compliments, but she didn't need compliments to know what she was capable of. The work speaks for itself.

Eli looked at his watch. "Looks like it's time to get started. The people seem like they're getting restless. I'm going to let Zachariah know he can start letting people in. Are you going to be okay over here?"

"Go ahead, I'll be fine. My feet are hurting, so I'm going to the seating area under the tent. That'll give me time to go through my emails. I need to confirm the cleaning crew will be here by six o'clock. We can't have this parking lot looking a mess tomorrow when we start services. Please make sure our greeters are having everyone fill out contact cards. They need to receive the completed cards prior to giving out tickets for the games and food."

Eli gave Maxine a wink and salute before taking off. Maxine's cell phone buzzed in her pocket. She pulled it out and read the message.

Jonathan: I want to see you.

Maxine: Can't today, church carnival.
Remember. Besides, it's the weekend.

Jonathan: Are you talking about the carnival my company Wen Wright Enterprises, sponsored by donating fifty thousand dollars?

Maxine: Yes.

Jonathan: Meet me at the spot in a couple of hours. Fat boy will be busy sucking up to the people trying to get them to become members of his church. I bet he won't even notice you're gone.

Jonathan was persistent in his pursuit.

Maxine: I told you I can't. I promise I'll make it up to you next week when I see you.

Maxine deleted the text thread before placing the phone back in her pocket. Since rekindling their romance, Jonathan had offered Maxine several monetary gifts. She refused each of them, noting Eli was meeting all her financial needs. When the need for corporate sponsorship arose for the carnival, Maxine casually mentioned it during one of their weekly trysts. A couple of days later, a check showed up in the church's post office box. Maxine felt no guilt about receiving money from Jonathan on behalf of the church.

Despite Jonathan's insistence, Maxine would not leave the carnival to meet him. Things between them were different this time around. He didn't have the power over her he once possessed. When they were together before, she depended on him for most of her financial needs. With that no longer being the case, Maxine decided she would make her own rules. Jonathan had no choice but to deal with it.

Maxine often threatened to end their affair, using the threat as leverage when they had a disagreement. Her threats were futile. Although Eli had lost a significant amount of weight, Maxine still preferred to be intimate with Jonathan. Her intimate moments with Eli were out of obligation. With Jonathan, it was desire.

"Sweetheart," Eli called to Maxine. "Come here, please. I have someone I want you to meet."

Maxine joined Eli, standing in front of a petite woman dressed in a gray suit. She immediately recognized the woman as the mayor of Chicago. A reporter and camera operator accompanied the mayor. Eli and Maxine walked around pointing out carnival attractions to their guests. They shook hands with a few of the attendees before settling into the sitting area.

"Pastor Clayton, I applaud you and your lovely wife. This community has historically been underserved. As mayor, it's my duty to look out for the well-being of all Chicagoans. When church and community leaders, such as yourselves, take the initiative to support our citizens through outreach programs, it not only helps the city, but I believe it also affects the world. I came today to let you know your church has the support of the City of Chicago. If you need help to get approval for any projects or permits, contact my office directly."

"Thank you, Madam Mayor. We are looking forward to partnering with you and the City of Chicago." Eli extended his hand to the mayor for a handshake. The group gathered for photos before parting ways.

Maxine put her arm around Eli's waist and gave him a gentle squeeze. "Wow, we are on our way. The mayor doesn't show up for everybody. Having the mayor of Chicago show up at our event is major. Our church is already making a buzz at city hall, and we haven't even had our first service yet. This is huge."

RASHIDA AND ALVIN ARRIVED AT THE CARNIVAL AND approached Eli and Maxine.

"Pastor Clayton," Alvin called out to Eli, extending his hand. "Man, I have to give it to you. This is nice. You've got games, prizes, and food. This is a full-fledged carnival. The only thing missing are the rides, but I don't hear anyone complaining. What I want to know is how you could do all of this and make it free? It's a first for me. I don't recall ever seeing anything like this done for free, and I've been around a long time."

"Man, it's by the grace of God, and the help of my beautiful wife." Eli kissed Maxine on the side of her head.

Rashida looked at Maxine and raised an eyebrow. "Look at you, doing big things, First Lady. I see you, boo."

Maxine noted the sarcasm in Rashida's comment. "Thank you. I try my best." She looked back and forth from Eli to Alvin. "We're going to let you guys talk. Me and Rashida are going to have a little girl chat."

Grabbing Rashida by the wrist, Maxine giggled and pulled her away from their men.

"Girl, if you don't let my wrist go," Rashida demanded. Her tone was playful, but she was not playing.

Once the ladies were at a safe distance from Eli and Alvin, Maxine peered at Rashida. "Rashi, what's wrong with you? Why do you keep throwing shade? Did I do something to you I'm not aware of?"

"What are you talking about? Ain't nobody throwing shade at you." Rashida folded her arms. "It must be your guilty conscience."

"I don't have a guilty conscience. I have done nothing wrong," Maxine shot back.

"Lies you tell. Remember this is me you're talking to. I know you better than anybody."

"You don't have to keep saying you know me. It goes both ways. We know each other. I don't know what has you acting so high and mighty now, but I'm getting bored with it."

"I'm not getting all high and mighty. Like I told you before, when you asked me if I would cover for you, I'm not about the nonsense. I don't have a heaven or hell to put you in. Your actions are yours alone. I just hope you know what you're doing."

"Where is all of this coming from? You and I have barely talked lately. Shoot, you and Alvin just arrived. I couldn't have made you mad that quick. You haven't been here a half hour, so what is it that has your panties in such a bunch?"

"You think I'm stupid, don't you? You want to know why I'm upset with you? There you have it. I'm far more intelligent than you give me credit for."

Shaking her head, Maxine raised her hands. "Look, I don't have time for you to be out here speaking in riddles. Either say what's on your mind, or get over it and let's enjoy this day."

"Oh, so you're seriously going to pretend like I don't know you're messing around with Jonathan again."

"Jonathan!" Maxine bellowed. "What in the world gave you

that idea?" Folding her arms tight across her chest, she continued, "Now I know you're tripping."

"Okay, I'm tripping. Let me clue you in on a few things. The day you and I went to the spa, I went to the back before you. When I got back there, they asked me what we wanted for lunch. I said I wasn't sure. I noticed you hadn't come to the back yet. Silly me, I figured you were paying the bill or taking care of some business or something, so I came up front to ask you. I saw you sitting in the corner talking to Jonathan. You didn't see me because you were too caught up in the lies he was telling you."

Rashida shifted her weight and put one hand on her hip. "Here I am thinking, this man is crazy. My girl ain't going to fall for his lies. I went into the dressing room and changed clothes. If you'll recall, the dressing room where we were told to put our belongings was exclusive. You and I were the only ones with a key. I finished my treatment a little early because my stomach started hurting. I came into the dressing room to get something out of my purse. That's when I realized your clothes weren't in there because you obviously never undressed."

"When we met for lunch and I saw you sitting there wearing the spa robe with your hair messed up, I was straight disgusted. I thought, Maxine is my best friend. How could I judge her? I kept waiting for you to confide in me, but you never did. I saw the guilt on your face. You looked like you genuinely felt bad. I figured that was punishment enough. You're my girl, so I let it go."

"Then you had the nerve to ask me to cover for you. After that, I knew the guilt you felt didn't last long. You were still seeing Jonathan, even after he dogged you the way he did. It's one thing to cheat and disrespect your husband, but to bring the mess to the church. I can't get with that."

Maxine thought for a moment before she responded. She couldn't deny anything Rashida said because it was all true.

Though the comment about the church had her puzzled. No one knew about the donation Jonathan made for the carnival but she and he. There was no way Rashida could have guessed. Maxine decided it was best to only address her comment about the church.

"You're right on most of what you said, but I have no clue what you're talking about concerning the church. Jonathan has nothing to do with this church."

"Really, Maxine? Jonathan has circled this block at least eight times since I've been here. I know it's him because I've never seen another car like his. Who else is going to ride through here in a Rolls Royce? Besides, he has a custom paint job on his car, so I know it's him."

"What!" Maxine looked around in a panic. She had been so busy focusing on the festivities, she didn't notice Jonathan's car. As if they had summoned him, Jonathan passed the church once again. This time, he beeped the horn. Maxine watched in horror until his car was out of view.

"Now who's tripping?" Rashida said, snapping her fingers in front of Maxine's face.

Maxine pulled the phone from her pocket and dialed Jonathan's number. She tapped her foot vigorously, waiting for him to pick up.

"What's up, baby?" Jonathan greeted after a few rings.

"I cannot believe you had the nerve to come up here after I told you I can't see you today. You're up here circling the block like a freaking mad man. I can't believe you, Jonathan." Maxine was livid. "Look, I can't do this with you. What we had is done. Do you hear me? It's over."

"Ah, nah, baby girl, that's where you're wrong. It's not over until I say it's over." Jonathan ended the call before Maxine could utter a reply.

Maxine slid the phone down her cheek. "Rashi," she said, stricken by panic. "Girl, I'm in trouble."

Rashida put her hands on her hips, looked Maxine in the eyes, and acknowledged, "You sure are."

Forty-One

The inaugural service of What a Mighty God Cathedral brought congregants in droves. As expected, several members from Pastor Scott's church joined Eli and Maxine in their new church. Eli's best friend, Zachariah, agreed to come aboard as the assistant pastor. Zachariah's wife served in the capacity of youth leader. The service flowed like that of a well-established ministry.

Maxine invited both Eli's parents and her parents over to their house for a celebratory dinner. Zachariah, his wife Sharna, Rashida, and Alvin rounded out the guest list. Daliah prepared a meal fit for royalty. To make the dinner flow seamlessly, Maxine hired a wait staff to serve the meal and tend to the guests.

"Service sure was nice today," Rose declared as the servers placed appetizers of Moroccan stuffed mushrooms, and steak and prosciutto skewers in front of each guest. "I enjoy your preaching style, Eli. Never thought I'd see the day when my daughter would be a pastor's wife. I thought she would be a big shot attorney. She's as smart as a whip." Rose took a sip of sparkling water. "You know what they say. If you want to make God laugh, tell him your plans."

Eli's mother spoke up, "I always knew Eli would be a preacher. Even as a child, he excelled at delivering speeches. Ooh, and let me tell you, Eli loved going to church. Now that brother of his is a different story, but Eli never fussed or complained about going. I thought it would change when he became a teenager or even at college, but nope, he remained true to his calling."

"And now here we are." Eli drew everyone's attention. He didn't want the mothers to get into the, my son, your daughter debate. The church resulted from both his and Maxine's hard work. "God knows my wife, and I didn't get here on our own. Had it not been for the love and dedication of all of you, and the church staff, today would not have been as successful."

"This is only the beginning," Maxine interjected. "We have some big plans in the works that will help the community and help grow the church."

"I can hardly wait for the basketball games to start," Rashida chimed in. "A lot of the children showed interest when you mentioned it before your sermon. By the time we left, the sign-up sheets in the welcome center were filled with the names of kids interested in trying out for the teams."

"I've been in contact with some of the other churches in the city. So far, I've found a few that have their own teams," Sharna added. "Based on the number of children we had to sign up, we will have more than enough to form multiple teams. We'll be able to have games where our teams play against each other, but it's going to be cool when we can play against other churches. The youth leader at Christ the True Vine was especially interested."

"Isn't that Pastor Maxwell Lee's church?" Alvin asked.

Maxine rolled her eyes. She and Rashida were the only ones who knew the history between Maxine and Maxwell. Her distaste for hearing his name seemingly went unnoticed by the dinner guests.

Rose got excited. “We know Pastor Lee very well. Maxine grew up with him. I’m still friends with his mother.”

“I didn’t know you knew Pastor Lee, sweetheart. You never mentioned it,” Eli said to Maxine. “Perhaps we can build a fellowship between his ministry and ours.”

“I never mentioned it because it wasn’t important. We were friends as kids. I haven’t communicated with him in a very long time.”

The servers brought the main course and conversations died down. The guests feasted on their choice of Beef Wellington or Chicken Marsala served with garlic roasted red potatoes and bacon wrapped asparagus.

“Man, this food is delicious,” Mr. Clayton acknowledged. “If that chef of yours is cooking meals like this, it’s no wonder you dropped that weight. Son, you look good.” He spoke between bites. “It’s a good thing, too. You’re going to need that extra energy pastoring a church. Based on today’s turn out, it appears the carnival idea was a hit. What else do you all have planned to sustain the membership? Most people will only attend if they feel like they’re getting something out of it.”

“You’re telling the truth there, Mr. Clayton,” Zachariah agreed. “We can hope the people are coming for the sermons and spiritual growth, but the reality is, many will come to see what they can get. They want to feel like the church is benefiting them.”

Interrupting the men, Maxine called out, “We’re raffling off a car in a couple of months. We could do it now, but we’re waiting until the church has been established for a little while. We don’t want people thinking we’re trying to buy members.”

Eli looked at Maxine in surprise. During one of their conversations, he casually mentioned to Maxine Pastor Scott’s idea of raffling off a vehicle. She said she thought it was a great idea and that they should do it, but he never agreed. The conversation hadn't gone any further. Now, she had put the idea out in front of their guests as if it was something they'd agreed on.

"Man, you're raffling off a car?" Alvin challenged. "That's crazy, you're the second pastor I heard mention the idea. I can't recall who the first one was."

"It was Pastor Scott," Zachariah chimed in. "I know because I heard him talking about it among some preachers." Zachariah cut his eyes at Eli.

The rebuke was not lost on Eli. He used his eyes to point at Maxine. His silent gesture was to inform his friend of the source of the stolen idea. Zachariah raised his chin in acknowledgment.

"You're giving away a car?" Rashida bellowed. "Dang. People will be flooding the church house hoping for a chance to win. The question is, will they stay after they don't win? Unless you're giving away a church full of cars." Rashida started laughing. "I can see it now, Maxine standing on the platform like Oprah talking about you get a car, you get a car."

"Nothing has been decided," Eli proclaimed. "My wife and I are still ironing out the details. As the pastor, my responsibility is to tend to the needs of the congregation spiritually first. I never want What a Mighty God Cathedral to be perceived as a church built on schemes or gimmicks. Serving the Lord is our top priority."

A hush fell over the room. Rashida looked at Maxine, raised an eyebrow, and mouthed, "This is going to be interesting."

Forty-Two

Three months later

"Man, your wife be wilding out." Zachariah plopped down in the leather chair opposite Eli's desk.

Eli sat back and tossed an ink pen on the desk. He stared at his friend with overwhelming curiosity. "What happened?"

"She has the leadership staff outraged. Apparently, she is micromanaging everybody. Maxine has her hands in everything. She gave a list of approved songs to the musicians and praise team leaders. The greeters received notification of an official dress code. Then the teaching staff was told to present lesson plans for the upcoming month by next Sunday to cover the full month."

Placing his head in his hands, Eli asked, "Why haven't I been notified of this?"

Zachariah sat up straight. "I'm notifying you now. My wife is so upset. It's going to take me a week to calm her down."

"Oh no, what did she say to Sharna?"

"The First Lady," Zachariah said like the words tasted bitter, "told my wife, all the youth activities must be approved by her at conception. She wants a detailed report of the proposed activity, any costs involved, staff and or volunteers needed, and an explanation of how the said activity will benefit the youth."

"Based on the examples you are giving; the requests don't sound unreasonable. We are building a ministry of excellence. You know that."

"I get the whole excellence thing. The problem everyone is having is not necessarily the request, it's the delivery. Anytime someone questions her, she asserts she's the first lady and what she says goes."

"Man, I don't know why Maxine is on this power trip. When we established the church, she told me she wanted to sit pretty and chill. The ministry has been running smoothly up to this point. Why is she shaking things up? I'll talk to her."

Zachariah stood. "Please do. I'd hate for you to lose valuable ministry staff over some foolishness. Remember, most of these positions are unpaid. It's a lot easier to keep the people you have happy, than it is to select and train an entire new staff. Sharna will not give up her position, but man, my wife is from the south side. She's not going to tolerate foolishness."

Eli stood to walk Zachariah out. "Thank you for letting me know. I didn't know any of this was going on. The good news is no one has quit. The situation is not beyond repair."

"Hold on, why are you rushing me out?" Zachariah asked, stopping just shy of the door.

"I have a meeting with Sister Marian. I've been counseling her. Man, that sister is going through with her husband. Please keep her in your prayers."

"You're not counseling her alone, are you?" Zachariah asked sincerely.

"Yes, of course. I want the members to know they can trust

me. With the stuff she's dealing with, she needs to know what she tells me is confidential."

Zachariah shook his head. "Counseling her alone is not a good idea. You need to have either your wife or another woman in the church to sit in on your counseling sessions. I'm telling you this out of love and concern. You're my friend and my pastor. I don't want to see you get wrapped up in a situation."

"Come on. You know me better than that. I would never make a move on a woman that's not my wife."

"I know it, and you know it, but you have a lot going for you. I'm not saying Sister Marian is not on the up and up, but all it takes is one false accusation to bring your entire world crashing down. Not just Sister Marian, any woman, for that matter."

"I hear you, man. Trust me, I got this. I'll keep what you said in mind."

"Don't just hear me. You need to listen. Warning comes before destruction."

"I got it. I appreciate your concern, I really do. Trust me on this." Eli patted Zachariah on the back and urged him out the door.

Being in both business and ministry, Eli understood his friend's concern. He knew Zachariah was only looking out for him. The advice his friend gave was sound advice, but Eli chose instead to trust his gut. If things went awry, he would make the necessary changes.

Returning to his desk, he picked up the phone to call Maxine. If she was creating a poor work environment for the church staff, he needed to nip it in the bud. Eli had noticed a change in his wife over the past couple of months, but he couldn't identify the source of her discontent. Whenever he asked her what was wrong, she waved it off. He wanted to make her happy, but Maxine was making it difficult.

Since starting the church, Eli divided his time between the dealership and the church. He was determined to give his all at both locations. As if a light bulb turned on in his brain, it occurred to him, Maxine may be acting out from the lack of attention he had shown her lately. Prior to the church launch, they spent time together talking and enjoying regular date nights. They were growing closer as a couple. Maxine had even started to not only return his affections, but she initiated her own. He was so busy with the church and dealership; he hadn't focused on intimacy in any form. Maxine hadn't complained, so he thought nothing of it… until now.

Light taps on the door prevented Eli from completing his call. "Come in," he called.

Sister Marian entered the office wearing a royal blue and white polka dot top. The scoop neckline revealed a rose tattoo on the right, just above her bust. White knit slacks revealed her curves, while doing little to mask her choice of underwear. Eli's head ached. In previous meetings, Marian had dressed modestly. A polar-opposite appearance from her current choice of dress.

Eli wondered if Zachariah was privileged to information concerning Sister Marian that he himself was not aware of. A wave of nausea at the thought of being wrongfully accused of inappropriate behavior swept over Eli, creating a mound of discomfort.

"Sister Marian, hello."

"Hey, Pastor Clayton," she answered in a singsong tone.

Eli's internal sensor buzzed like a biohazard alarm. He stood before she could reach the guest chairs. "Did we have an appointment today?"

"Yes, Pastor. Last week before I left, I told you I needed to change my appointment to today instead of this upcoming Thursday. You said it wouldn't be a problem."

"My apologies, Sister. I'm not feeling my best." He grabbed

his stomach. "I'm dealing with some bad nausea. I'm heading home early today."

"Oh, Pastor, is there something I can do to help?" Marian asked, continuing towards him.

Eli held up his hand, halting her steps. "No. I'll be fine. If it's a stomach bug, I don't want you to catch it. I'm sorry about today's appointment. I'll have my assistant contact you to reschedule. In the meantime, I will continue to pray for you and your husband."

Marian was hesitant. "Oh, okay, Pastor. I hope you feel better soon." She turned and walked towards the door, just as Maxine entered, unannounced.

Forty-Three

"HEY, FIRST LADY," SISTER MARIAN SANG AS SHE sashayed out the door.

"Marian," Maxine responded. "What's going on here?" she asked, looking from Marian to Eli. Maxine scanned Marian's outfit before she turned and allowed her eyes to linger on Eli.

"I was just leaving," Marian replied snickering and glancing over her shoulder at Eli. "I'll see you next week, Pastor. Take care of yourself. We need you healthy and strong." She walked out and closed the door behind her.

Blood drained from Eli's face as he stood stoic. "Maxine, what are you doing here? I mean, I was just about to call you."

Maxine marched to her husband's desk. "I bet you were. What the..."

"Before you get upset, it's not what you think," Eli interrupted. "There is nothing going on between me and Sister Marian. I've been counseling her concerning her marriage."

"Sure you have. Is that what they call screwing around now? Counseling, yeah right. Eli, you don't know me. I will shut this place down."

"You are getting yourself upset over nothing. All this extra you're doing is pointless. I've told you there's nothing going on between me and her. Let it go. It's done and over. I'm glad you're here. I need to talk to you anyway concerning church business."

"Have you lost your mind?" Maxine asked, pointing her finger in Eli's face. "We're not done until I say we're done. You must be crazy." Maxine flailed her arms. "I made you, Pastor Clayton. Did you forget? You wouldn't have any of this if it wasn't for me. The same way I built you up, I can break you down. In a heartbeat. Now I suggest you call that little whore of yours and end whatever this is you think you have going on."

Maxine stormed out of the office, slamming the door against the wall. She went to her office and retrieved her phone and handbag. Exiting the church, she bumped into Rashida, almost knocking her to the ground.

"Dang, girl. What's wrong with you?" Rashida asked. Her forehead wrinkled in anger. "You almost knocked me down. Where are you going, anyway? I thought you wanted me to meet you up here."

"Not now, Rashi," Maxine replied. Her breathing mimicking a runner after a sprint.

"Nope. See, what I'm not about to do is let you leave upset like this. You are not in the frame of mind to drive. You'll pull out of here all mad, not paying attention to traffic and end up causing an accident, killing yourself or somebody else."

"Why do you have to be so dramatic?"

"I'm just saying, the look you have on your face right now is not safe. You already almost knocked me down, and you were walking then. I can only imagine what the outcome would be if you were in a car." Rashida pulled on Maxine's arm. "Come on, let's go for a ride. You obviously need to vent, or something. I'm the one you can vent to. You definitely can't tell anybody up in there." She pointed to the church building.

"Okay, Fine."

Maxine had barely sat down in Rashida's car before the tears fell.

"What's wrong?" Rashida reached over and grabbed Maxine's hand. She backed out of the parking space and drove away from the church, giving her friend the privacy she needed. She drove a safe distance from the church and pulled into a store parking lot.

"Eli is cheating on me," Maxine cried. Her tears flowed with no sign of easing.

"Who's cheating? Eli? No way. He loves you way too much to cheat on you."

"I walked in on him and Sister Marian today at the church. That's the reason I was so upset when I was leaving." Maxine dabbed at her eyes with a tissue she found in Rashida's glove box.

"Let me get this straight. Eli was sleeping with Sister Marian at the church, and you walked in on them. This is unbelievable. Does anybody respect the church anymore?"

"No, Rashida. I didn't walk in on them in the act. I walked into his office unannounced, and they were standing there looking guilty. She was dressed all seductive, and he was standing there looking stupid. He had the nerve to tell me he was counseling her, like I'm supposed to believe him."

"Were there any lingering scents in the room?" Rashida asked, bucking her eyes.

"Scents?" Maxine looked dumbfounded.

"You know what I'm talking about, Maxine. Don't play dumb."

"No."

"Girl, wipe your face. You and I both know your man ain't cheating on you." Rashida grabbed several tissues from the box and pressed them into Maxine's hand.

Accepting the tissues, Maxine wiped her eyes, face, and chin before blowing her nose.

"Ew, you're gross." Rashida teased.

"Shut up."

"If you're done, we can get to the truth of what's really going on with you."

Maxine turned and looked at her friend. "What are you talking about?"

"You know I'm going to keep it real with you. I'm probably the only one who will tell you the truth. For the past couple of months, you have been a straight. I'm not going to say it, but you know what I'm thinking."

"I know you didn't," Maxine shot back cutting her eyes at Rashida.

"No, I didn't, but you and I both know I could have. You're walking around the church treating people like they are soldiers in your army. You've been making up crazy rules and some more stupid junk. I'm telling you because you're my friend. People are going to dip out if you don't relax. I know you don't want things to go that way, but I'm telling you they will. You don't know how many people have left churches they like because of a crazy first lady."

"I don't care."

"Yes, you do. You can tell that lie to somebody that doesn't know you."

Maxine pressed her back against the seat and closed her eyes. "Have I been that bad?"

"Yep, you sure have. It started after you ended things with Jonathan. The longer you've been away from him, the worse you've gotten. I thought with Eli losing so much weight, and looking decent, I might add, you would focus your attention on him. Allowing him to take care of you, physically and emotionally. It appears it's not the case. You act like a woman in desperate need of some TLC."

Tears formed once again. Maxine struggled to keep them at

bay. "I won't lie. I miss Jonathan. He and I have history. When I was seeing him, I knew it was going to be consistent. Every week we made plans to see each other." Maxine paused and shook her head. "But ending things with Jonathan is not what has me upset."

"Then what is it?"

"Eli is looking so much better since he lost the weight and got his skin together. With his sexy new appearance, along with the way he treats me, I've become attracted to him."

"That's good, girl."

"No, it's not. Eli has been so focused on building this stupid church, he's forgotten all about me. I've done all kinds of stuff trying to get his attention. None of it works. By the time he gets home, he is too tired for anything... including me."

"Aww, Maxine. You're falling for your husband. How sweet."

"Rashi, don't make fun. It's not funny."

"I'm not being funny. I think it's sweet. Especially with the way all of this started. I can see why not having his attention now that you want it, is hurtful. Why don't you talk to him?" Rashida patted Maxine's hand.

"When you started talking about being a pastor's wife, I was hoping you were joking. Most people don't realize the drama first ladies go through. As a pastor's wife, you're forced to share your husband with a whole congregation of people. That's not easy for any woman. I'm your friend, but I can't tell you what it's like being a first lady. Maybe you should reach out to some other pastor's wives. You're good at organizing stuff. You could start a support group or something. As your friend, I'm asking you to please get some help, and stop taking your drama out on the church leaders."

"That's a good idea. How did you get so smart?"

"I've always been smart. You just couldn't see it, because you can't see past yourself."

"Dog. That's harsh."

"No, girlfriend. That's real. One thing I know for sure, you can't spend as much time in church as you do and it not rub off on you. Now please, do yourself and everyone else a favor. Talk to your husband. Let him know how you feel."

Forty-Four

Eli was furious. He couldn't believe Maxine would talk to him the way she had at the church. He had been nothing but good to her. There was nothing she asked for that he didn't attempt to give her. The things she said to him were cruel. Growing up, Eli's mother always told him and his brother, if you want to know what people think about you, get them angry and they will tell you.

Unfortunately, for Eli, in this case, his mother was right. His lungs filled with air as he turned the doorknob and walked inside the home he shared with Maxine. He mentally prepared himself for another verbal attack. Maxine had gotten the upper hand over him earlier because they were at the church. As the pastor, Eli didn't want to present himself before the church members in an unfavorable light.

Following Maxine's angry departure from the church, Eli spent the next hour apologizing to the staff for her behavior. He was furious. When news of the outburst reached Zachariah, he immediately returned to Eli's office. Eli placed his keys on the counter, pulled a bottle of water from the fridge, and reflected on their conversation.

"Eli, what's going on, man? You got these folks running around here gossiping like it's a paying gig. Somebody said you were in here with a woman and your wife caught you. I shot that down when they brought it to me because I know you. It hasn't been that long since I left your office. What gives?"

"Zach, as much as I hate to admit it, you were right. Sister Marian came up in here dressed quite seductive. Far less modest than she previously had. My internal radar went off, so I canceled the meeting. She was leaving when Maxine came in. My wife took one look at Marian and acted a plain fool. She wasn't willing to hear anything I said. I'm sure nobody could hear what she was saying to me, so that's not what garnered attention. When she left, she slammed the door against the wall and got the gossip bees buzzing."

"I told you, you didn't need to be in here by yourself with Sister Marian. Even with good intentions, too much could go wrong. As far as your wife is concerned, knowing her the way I do, I'm sure she was furious. Given the circumstances, I'm going to assume you didn't get to mention the issues with the church staff to her."

"You have got to be kidding me."

Zachariah raised his hands in surrender. "My bad, man. It's too soon. I'll talk to you later." He left Eli's office without protest.

Eli reflected on the day and realized some things could have been avoided had he listened to Zachariah. His admittance didn't justify Maxine's actions, but he could see how his actions triggered hers. Eli felt there was much he didn't know about his wife. Their courtship was brief. Shortly after getting married, they started the church. He hadn't taken the time to get to know the woman he married.

As an associate minister at Pastor Scott's church, Eli heard rumors about Sister Scott being upset because she felt her husband gave too much attention to the church and not enough to her. Although he and Maxine hadn't been in ministry long, he wondered if she was feeling the same way. They had been so busy focusing on the church, Eli had forgotten they were still newlyweds. He considered perhaps compassion was what his wife needed, not rebuke.

Moving through the house, Eli found Maxine in the theater curled up on a recliner. She was watching a classic movie featuring Richard Pryor, Redd Foxx, and Eddie Murphy. The tension in the room was thick.

"Hey, sweetheart," Eli greeted. "Do you mind if I join you?"

"Suit yourself," Maxine replied, refusing to look at him.

Eli sat in the recliner next to Maxine. He wanted to start a conversation, but decided it was best not to interrupt the movie.

The movie ended and Maxine stood to leave. Placing his hand on her wrist, Eli gently guided her back down.

"Please, can we talk?"

"What do you want to talk about? I said all I wanted to say."

"You said some harsh things. I won't lie. It took all the God I have in me not to retaliate. I realized my reaction would either make things worse or set the tone for healing. I could have run after you or said ugly words, but for what? It wouldn't have solved anything."

"What did you expect? I walk into my husband's office, who also happens to be the pastor, and find this woman with a shirt cut so low it was showing her bust tattoo. Plus, she was wearing pants you could see straight through. You and her in the office alone, looking all guilty. Then she had the nerve to be smirking at me. I'm still new to this church stuff, but nothing about that situation looked right. You hurt me badly. I'm not that saved. In return to being hurt, I said things I knew would hurt you."

"Did you mean the things you said?" Eli wanted to know. "You came across like I'm some pet project of yours."

"Be for real. Like I said, you hurt me, so I retaliated. You said you were done like your word was law, and I had no opinion when you were the one caught in a compromising position. One to which I'm still not sure isn't what it seemed."

"You're right. Sweetheart, I apologize. I can understand how things may have appeared. You're the only woman for me. I would never do anything to intentionally hurt you. Let me make it up to you."

"Make it up to me how?" Maxine bore into Eli, waiting for an explanation.

"I've been so busy being pastor, I haven't taken enough time being husband." Eli pulled Maxine into his arms and kissed her on each cheek. Tonight, I'm putting the dealership and the church aside. This night is all about you. My beautiful wife.

Forty-Five

"UM, I GUESS SOMEBODY MADE UP," RASHIDA TEASED. "You and Eli are walking around here acting like real newlyweds."

"We *are* newlyweds," Maxine countered.

"I'm not hating, honey child, I'm celebrating." Rashida embraced her friend. "You genuinely look happy. In all the years I've known you, I don't believe I've ever seen it. I mean, you've been happy at times, but there was always an underlying sadness. Now I'm seeing the happy without the sadness. I love it. Happiness looks good on you."

"Don't be in here trying to make me cry."

"If *you* start crying, I know something ain't right."

"Don't worry, I won't give you the satisfaction of seeing my tears twice. Enough about me. What's up with you and Alvin? I'm glad to see the brother stuck around. When you first met him, I thought he was going to be a one and done. I didn't expect you two to hang together this long. You must be putting it down."

"Nope, I'm not putting anything down. Alvin is a good man. He's a pastor who practices what he preaches. I'm enjoying getting to know him on an intellectual level. It's nice having a man who sees me for more than my body."

"I hear you, girl. You never know what your relationship with Alvin will lead to. We may one day be bestie first ladies."

"Who knows?" Rashida hunched her shoulders. "Speaking of first ladies, how are things going with your pastor's wives support group?"

Maxine grabbed her bottle of water off the counter and took a sip. "I wouldn't call us a support group. It sounds too much like AA or something. I think we're more of a social club. We get together for lunch once a month and just talk. Sometimes we share ideas we think will benefit the other ministries. Other times we have a no church talk rule. It depends on the mood of the meeting. You will not believe who's in the group."

"You know I don't like guessing games. You may as well tell me."

"Man, you take all the fun out of stuff. You're a whole fun sucker."

The ladies burst into laughter.

"Girl, you're crazy. Now come on, stop stalling. Tell me who you're talking about."

"Amirah Lee."

Rashida frowned. "Amirah Lee. Why does her name sound familiar?"

"Her name sounds familiar because she is Maxwell Lee's wife. Let me tell you, she is catching the blues. I thought we had drama at What a Mighty God Cathedral. It's nothing compared to what she deals with at Christ the True Vine."

"Like what?" Rashida got excited.

"It's not for me to say. Maybe if you and Alvin jump the broom one day, I'll invite you into the club and you can hear for yourself."

"Tell me. You can't build up a story and then change the

subject." Rashida put her hands on her hips and puffed out her cheeks.

Maxine laughed. "You can stand there looking like a blowfish all you want. I'm still not going to tell you. All I'm going to say is, please pray for her and Maxwell."

"Does she know you and Maxwell used to date?"

"No, she doesn't, and I plan to keep it right there. She knows we grew up together, but she does not know about our adult interactions. We weren't intimate, so it doesn't matter, anyway."

Eli came behind Maxine and wrapped his arms around her waist. He kissed her on the neck. "What are you ladies over here talking about?"

Leaning into Eli, Maxine replied. "I was telling Rashida what a blessing the first ladies' meetings have been to me."

"Oh, okay. When you're done, can you join us on the patio? I want to share something with the group."

Maxine looked at her husband curiously. After the situation with Sister Marian and Maxine's actions toward the church leaders, they agreed with church business they wouldn't keep secrets. Maxine couldn't imagine what news Eli had to share that she hadn't been privy to.

"We'll be out in a moment." Maxine scrambled around the kitchen, straightening up, prolonging the time to join Eli on the patio. Rashida had already gone outside. Maxine knew everyone was waiting for her. She tried to mentally prepare for whatever the news was Eli had to share. She'd heard enough stories from the other first ladies to know some pastors had a habit of allowing their wives to hear important information along with the congregation. The wives had to grin and bear it to save face. Maxine hoped this wouldn't be one of those moments.

Unable to stall any longer, she went out to the patio to join everyone else. When Eli saw her approaching, he beckoned her over to join him.

"As you all know, it has always been my wife's and my desire to build a community center to serve the community and our church family. The community center will feature free meals, a state-of-the-art media center, and gym. I'm pleased to announce, because of a sizable donation, we are moving forward with the community center project."

The group clapped and yelped. Eli gave Maxine a gentle squeeze. She smiled in response, but the smile didn't reach her eyes.

Once the festivities were over, and the guests had departed, Maxine snuggled close to her husband. She was grateful for the alone time when she could speak freely. Not wanting to come across as demanding, she turned up the charm.

"Long day, huh?" she said, rubbing Eli on the back.

"Yeah, but it was a good day. It's nothing like getting together with our inner circle. The people we know are supporting us. Those who want to see us thrive. Like Pastor Alvin, for example. We're both pastors, but with us, it's never about competition. We realize there are enough people in this city for both of us to reach. Plenty of lives to impact."

"Do you still talk to Pastor Scott? I don't hear you mention him much. It seems since you came from his ministry, he would be one of the first to support you."

Eli caressed Maxine's cheek. "I'd hoped to maintain a fellowship with Pastor Scott when we left to start the ministry. Unfortunately, things haven't gone in that direction. I've reached out to him a few times, but to no avail. See, when we left, so did the financial support I contributed regularly."

"If he's upset with you for leaving, then he's really going to have a fit when you build the community center."

"Why do you think he'll be upset about the community center?" Eli asked.

"Didn't you tell me he wanted to build a community center? The center was the reason for the car raffle, wasn't it?"

"I'd forgotten about that. See, sweetheart, this is why we make a great team. When I'm slipping or forget something, I can count on you to remember. That's why I love you." Eli moved to kiss Maxine, but she eased away.

"Eli," she called in a sultry tone.

"Yes."

"How much was this sizable contribution you mentioned earlier? Better yet, who is the person who would make such a large contribution? Was it your dad?"

"No, it wasn't Dad. It's a guy by the name of Ernest Livengood."

"What kind of name is Livengood? Is it even a real name, and why did I have to find out about this along with everyone else?"

"Yes, it is. I checked him out. He seems to be legit. Even if he wasn't legit, the check he donated was. I hadn't mentioned it, because if it was some type of scam, it wouldn't have been worth bringing up. It's not every day a church receives a check for three hundred fifty thousand dollars."

"So, you waited until we were in front of all our friends to tell me? When did you get this check?"

"I received it last week at the church. The letter was addressed to me directly. When I saw the check, I contacted the church's accountant. He handled it from there. While we were here with the team earlier, the accountant called me and informed me the check had cleared. I wanted to surprise you. I felt the best way to do that was to make the announcement in front of our friends."

Maxine wasn't convinced. She hadn't been in church much throughout her life, so she wasn't familiar with the inner workings of things. She'd heard of anonymous donors giving to charities, but this all seemed too good to be true. Call it woman's intuition or paranoia. Either way, something didn't feel right.

"Let me get this straight. This man, who you don't know, sent a random check to you at the church for three hundred fifty thousand dollars, and he's not asking for anything in return? He doesn't want his name on the building, or a library named after him, nothing? Sounds suspect to me."

Eli pulled Maxine into his arms and kissed her head. "That brain of yours is probably smoking from being overworked. God blesses His people. Relax and see this as the blessing it is. Mr. Livengood hasn't asked to have any part of the building named after him. In the letter, he said he would like to meet us to thank us in person for the work we are doing in the community. He's not even asking to go to lunch or dinner. He'd like to meet with us at the church."

"When is this meeting supposed to take place?"

"Now that the check has cleared, I'll have the administrative assistant set it up. Alright, enough church talk. I want to spend some time with my beautiful wife. Come here and let me love on you."

Maxine surrendered to her husband's embrace, but her heart wasn't there. The entire situation was bazaar. She didn't know who Ernest Livengood was. However, something was fishy. She couldn't put her finger on it, but Maxine was determined to find out. No matter what.

Forty-Six

"Where is this woman?" Eli spoke aloud. He'd asked Maxine to be prompt for their meeting with Ernest Livengood, but as usual, she was running late. The meeting was being held at the church two hours before Bible study. Eli selected a time that wouldn't interfere with Mr. Livengood's work schedule. Eli also planned to invite the gentleman to stay for the service following their meeting.

It was ten minutes before the meeting was scheduled to start and still no word from Maxine. Eli rubbed his head and took a deep, cleansing breath. If Maxine was late, he wouldn't make a big deal of it. Her absence would give him and Ernest the opportunity to talk. Eli loved his wife, but he didn't care for her propensity to be overly vocal.

Eli's desk phone beeped, notifying him of an internal call. He pressed the speaker button to answer his assistant.

"Pastor Clayton, Mr. Ernest Livengood is here to see you. Shall I show him in?"

"Yes, please. Oh, has my wife arrived?"

"I haven't seen her yet," the assistant replied.

"That's fine. I'm sure she'll be joining us shortly. In the meantime, please see our guest to my office."

The door cracked and Eli stood to greet the generous donor.

"Pastor Clayton, thank you so much for inviting me. I've been looking forward to this meeting for a long time."

"Is that so?" Eli gave a curt response as recognition of his guest registered. "What are you doing here? My appointment is with Ernest Livengood. Not you."

Eli's guest stepped further into the room and took a seat across from him. He left his hat on. "Yes, I know. Ernest Livengood and I are the same. Perhaps I should formally introduce myself. Most people know me as Jonathan Freeman." Jonathan extended his hand to Eli for a handshake.

Eli folded his hands in response. "I'm aware of who you are. The question is, what are you doing here?"

"Oh, come on." Jonathan sat back and crossed his legs. "Is this any way to treat the man who donated three hundred and fifty thousand dollars to your church? No, wait. Let me correct that. I believe the total donation to date has been four hundred thousand. I could check with my accountant, but I'm sure the numbers are correct."

"The check we received was in the amount of three hundred fifty thousand."

"Yes, it was, but when you add the fifty thousand my company, Wen Wright Enterprises, donated for your little carnival, the total easily comes to four hundred thousand."

Rolling his eyes in disgust, Eli was thrown off guard. "Man, what is your issue? Maxine told me about her wrongful termination from your law firm. Are these little donations of yours your way of paying her back?" He clinched his jaw.

"Is that what she told you?" Jonathan adjusted himself. "The better question is, is that all she told you about me?"

"She told me all I needed to know. My wife no longer works

for you. Therefore, she has no further connection to you. Your donations to the church won't change that. If you thought your donations would give you some kind of power over me or my wife, you're wrong. I can write you a check right now to fix that theory."

"Nah, there's no need for any check writing. Keep your coins." Jonathan ran his fingers along the rim of his hat. "I've always taken care of my women. You know Maxine can be a bit high maintenance. I don't care, because I can afford to treat her the way she deserves to be treated. She told me you have a couple dollars. Since she decided she didn't need the money for herself anymore, donating it to the church was the next best thing. Maxine didn't want you financing this place," Jonathan waved his hands around, "out of your pocket."

"Your woman?" Eli stood. Church or no church, he was ready to knock this man to the floor. Eli spared Jonathan the first time he disrespected Maxine, but there was nothing but space and opportunity this time.

"Sit down, man. You're supposed to be a pastor. Besides, don't let this gray hair fool you. I can take you down without a blink." Jonathan waved his hands in a sweeping motion. "There's no need for violence. I get you're upset, but you need to understand. Maxine has been my woman for a long time. It wasn't until she cut a fool and started messing around with you that I had to show her who I am. I kicked her butt out of my condo and fired her. After a while I missed my sweet thang, so I took her back."

Jonathan pushed his index finger into his temple. "Think about it. From one man to another. Do you honestly think I would drop money like this on a woman who isn't giving me something in return? The week we spent in Maui a few months ago was unforgettable. The main reason I've stuck with Maxine for as long as I have is because she knows what I like. She'll do what my wife won't without prompting. I got her trained like that."

The office door opened just as Eli walked around the desk.

"I'm sorry I'm late. I got stuck in traffic." Maxine stepped quickly towards Eli and a man in a hat. Eli cut his eyes at her, causing her to slow her steps. As she advanced further into the room, the smell of Azēl filled her nostrils. She suddenly felt paralyzed. Maxine couldn't move further if she tried.

Jonathan turned around and sneered at her.

Looking back and forth from Eli to Jonathan, Maxine felt queasy. "Jonathan what... what are you doing here?" she stuttered.

"This here is Mr. Ernest Livengood," Eli spat as if he was spewing venom.

"Hey, baby girl, come on in here and sit your sexy self down. I was about to tell fat boy about our week in Maui. I thought he would enjoy hearing some of our pillow talk."

Maxine slapped Jonathan with all the strength she could muster. He back handed her in response.

Eli lunged forward, knocking Jonathan to the floor. His hat went flying across the room. "Don't you ever put your hands on my wife."

Blood splatter hit the wall from Jonathan's busted lip. He scrambled to his feet, wiping his mouth. "Your wife," Jonathan yelled. "You don't have a wife. Your marriage is a joke. You were convenient. How else would a tub of lard like you get a woman like Maxine? Don't fool yourself into thinking those couple of pounds you lost made a difference."

"Get out of here," Eli threatened, lunging toward Jonathan once more.

"This isn't over. I will bury you before it's done." Jonathan grabbed his hat and stumbled out the door, dabbing his bloody lip with a handkerchief.

Forty-Seven

With tears in her eyes, Maxine jumped up and ran to Eli with her arms extended. "Eli, baby, I'm sorry."

He held up his hand. "Stop. Don't touch me."

"Please," Maxine inched toward him. "Let me explain."

With open palms, Eli placed his hands on Maxine's shoulders. "Let you explain," he barked. "It seems your lover has done enough explaining for the both of you."

"He's not my lover. You have to believe me."

"Believe you!" Eli let out a laugh that sounded more like a howl. "You must be kidding me." Eli backed away from Maxine and turned to face the window. "You want me to believe you, the same way you believed me when I told you there was nothing going on between me and Sister Marian? The difference is nothing happened between me and her. I was her pastor. I counseled her, that's it. You lied to me. God only knows how many times. I don't even want to think about how many times you left his bed and came to mine."

"Eli, I love you. Please, can we talk about this?" Maxine grabbed his arm and turned him to face her.

Tears moistened Eli's face. "You love me. Wow, that's rich. Do you know how long I've waited to hear you say those words? It's unfortunate. After today, I believe it to be another one of your lies. I don't want to share a bed with you tonight. I don't even want to be in the same house as you."

"That's ridiculous. Baby, come on. You can't go by what Jonathan said. Common sense should tell you I'm not involved with him. Why do you think he did all this?"

"Oh, so now, along with all the other insults you and your man hurled at me, you're also saying I lack common sense. I'm not putting you off the property, but I don't want you in my house. Do us both a favor and have your stuff moved back to the guesthouse by the time I get home."

"Wait a minute. You don't mean that. I get it. You're upset, but you're taking things too far."

"I mean every word I've spoken. You can tell your boyfriend not to worry. Every dirty penny he donated to this church will be returned to him. I'm done with this." Eli picked up his keys and cell phone from the desk and walked away. Maxine tried to follow, but stopped when Eli slammed the door in her face.

Maxine pulled her phone from her purse, located Jonathan's phone number, and pressed the button to connect the call.

"Baby girl," Jonathan called out in a tone like the character Jerome on the Martin Lawrence sitcom. "I knew you'd be calling. That husband of yours better watch his back. By the time I'm done with him, he's going to need government assistance. I'm going to make sure he is penniless. Yeah, and that little church he's so proud of will burn to the ground."

"I can't believe you came here and did all of this. The fact you would go to these lengths because I broke things off with you is unbelievable. You lied to Eli and made him think we're still involved. I hate you, Jonathan. If you even think about bothering us again, everything you spoke concerning my husband will be done to you and your family. Trust me, you really don't want to make that move. I may be prim and proper, but I know people that can get things done. I wouldn't try me if I were you."

"Your threats are falling on deaf ears. If you think I'm letting this go, you're dumber than I thought. You and that tub of lard you married had better watch your backs. I mean it."

"Try me if you want to Jonathan Freeman. The next visitor that shows up at your house won't be as nice as Stella."

Maxine disconnected the call and left the church. She passed by the sanctuary on her way out. It sounded like Eli was teaching Bible study. Maxine dropped her head and exited the church.

At home, Maxine packed her belongings between tears. She couldn't believe Eli told her to leave. She was grateful he allowed her to move back to the guesthouse. Being married without a prenuptial agreement, Maxine knew she had rights to their home. She could fight Eli about making her move out, but she didn't want to. As much as she hated to admit the truth, she believed she deserved the treatment she was receiving. Rashida was right. Eli was a good man. He deserved a good woman. Maxine believed she could be that woman, but after the day's activities, the chance of mending her marriage was unlikely. Reconciliation would take a miracle.

Forty-Eight

THE SOUND OF A RINGING PHONE BROUGHT MAXINE running into the bedroom. She stumbled over a pile of clothes, trying to get to the device before the ringing stopped. The bed broke her fall. Quickly picking up the phone, she hoped the nightmare was ending. She dropped her head when she read the name on the display. Disappointment moistened her eyes with tears. Maxine allowed the phone to ring until the call transferred to voicemail.

With her head in her hands, Maxine sat on the bed, trembling. Every time she thought she had a handle on crying, the tears began again. She pulled tissues from a box on her side of the bed until she exhausted the supply. Once again, the phone rang. Maxine pressed *ignore*. After repeating the routine three additional times, the caller gave up and sent a text message.

> Rashida: What's going on, Maxine? I didn't see you at church, which is unusual, and Eli is looking all disheveled. Call me now. Let me know you're good. I'm worried about you.

Rashida attempted another call after sending the text. Just as before, Maxine ignored it. She didn't want to talk to Rashida. Maxine didn't want to talk to anyone, except Eli. She had finally gotten to a place of happiness and peace. Life was good and then Jonathan came and ruined it all. Maxine was so angry, she wished Jonathan dead.

Feeling defeated, Maxine yelled out in agony. For the first time in her life, she had fallen in love. She knew in her heart the way she treated Eli in the beginning was wrong. Somehow along the way, her heart got involved, causing her plan to use him for money and status to fall apart. Maxine had experienced pain before, but it was nothing like the pain she felt now.

Faced with losing everything, Maxine had to be honest with herself. Eli was generous by offering to let her live in the guesthouse, but she couldn't do it. Being so close to the man she loved, and not being able to be with him, would be unbearable. She gathered the last of her belongings and loaded her car. In tears, she drove until she arrived at the last place she ever thought she'd end up.

Maxine sat in the car, gripping the steering wheel. The more she tried to stop crying, the more the tears fell. She picked up her phone to call Eli, but reconsidered. Maxine figured she was the last person he wanted to talk to. In sorrow, she laid her head on the steering wheel. Taps on the passenger side window startled her.

"What's going on? Why are you out here like this? Are you crying?" Rose stepped around to the driver's side and pulled on the door handle.

Pushing the button to unlock the car door, Maxine allowed her mother access.

"Come on in the house, baby." Rose stepped aside so Maxine could exit the car. Enclosing Maxine in the warmth of her embrace, Rose helped her into the house. "Let me get you something to drink."

Maxine adjusted the throw pillows and took a seat on the ivory French Provincial sofa her mom had since Maxine's childhood. She outlined the ornate wood carvings in the sofa's arm with her finger. The wood was polished to a high shine. There was so much nostalgia in her mother's living room. Maxine felt like she was once again a teenager waiting to explain to her mother what happened at school.

The light rattling of glass alerted Maxine to her mother's return. "Here we go," Rose said, handing Maxine a cup of chamomile tea. She took a seat beside Maxine and patted her daughter on the knee.

"Mama," Maxine cried as she attempted to explain her dilemma between sniffles.

"Hush, now. Take your time and enjoy your tea. It'll calm your nerves. Something obviously has you upset. There's no rush. You can tell me when you're ready."

Maxine nodded, blew into the cup, then took a sip. The two sat in silence until Maxine consumed the entire cup. She turned to her mother with the humbleness of a child. Tears welled in her eyes. "Mama, I messed up."

Rose sat her cup down, moved closer to her daughter, and rubbed Maxine's back. "It's okay, I'm sure whatever it is, it's not that bad."

"Yes, it is. I hurt Eli and I can't fix it."

Gripping her chest, Rose cried, "Oh my, God. Please tell me you're not saying you physically hurt him."

"No, not physically. I'm not that crazy. Eli is a big man." Maxine told her mother the entire story of her involvement with Jonathan. She shared her desire to marry a preacher and how Eli fit into her plan.

"Let me get this straight." Rose began not hiding her

annoyance. "You targeted this man to fulfill some God forsaken plan to marry a preacher?"

"No, Mama. Our meeting was organic. We met at a department store. We didn't even exchange names or anything. Neither of us thought we would ever see each other again. After the initial meeting, the other times we met were completely random. I liked him as a person."

"But not as a husband?" Rose countered.

"Not at first. I didn't expect to fall in love with Eli. The more time I spent getting to know him, the more I *wanted* to be with him. His appearance was no longer a factor. Mama, you have to believe me. Eli and I are good together. Now I've lost him because of a man I want nothing to do with. Eli said I could live in the guesthouse, but I can't live that close to him without living with him," Maxine sobbed.

Rose pulled Maxine into her arms. "You can stay here with me and Pops until you and Eli work things out. Right now, he's understandably upset. I've been with the two of you. Your husband loves you. He'll come around. Keep praying. God will work it out."

Forty-Nine

"SEVEN BALL, CORNER POCKET." ELI USED HIS POOL stick to point to the slot he was targeting. He aimed at the cue ball and took the shot with added force.

"Whoa, man, watch out," Zachariah yelled, jumping out of the way of the flying ball. He slammed his stick down on the pool table and folded his arms across his chest. "Look, you can't continue to avoid talking about the obvious. The church members may be afraid to talk to you, but I'm not. We've been boys a long time and I won't sit back and watch you self-destruct."

Eli stepped away from the pool table and retrieved a bottle of water from the mini fridge. He removed the cap from the bottle and turned it up, downing half the contents in a single gulp.

"Dude, don't start with me. I'm not in the mood for this tonight."

"You may not be in the mood to hear what I have to say, but I'm not leaving until I tell you what's on my mind. You have been moping around here for the past two weeks. The church members are not dumb. You were in Bible study a couple of weeks ago looking crazy. Your wife wasn't present, and now neither of you have been to the church since."

Zachariah helped himself to a bottle of water. "You better be glad your assistant loves you enough to keep her mouth closed to the members. She was there the night you beat that guy down in your office. I found out about it, because she confided in me to come clean his blood off the wall. You've been going down since. Look at you, sitting here unshaved, and eating all this junk food. You have isolated yourself in this house, not talking to anybody. You haven't even been to the dealership. I'm worried about you."

"You don't have to worry about me. I'm fine." Eli turned up a bag of potato chips, dropping crumbs on his shirt.

"Man, stop this." Zachariah snatched the bag from Eli and tossed the chips into the trash.

Eli jumped up and moved towards Zachariah.

"What? You going to jump on me now? Man, get a hold of yourself."

Dropping his head, Eli sat down on a bar stool. He was tired of fighting. Although he had no intention of hitting Zachariah, he wanted the pain he was feeling to end. He just didn't know how to get there. Feeling defenseless, Eli confided in his best friend.

"Man, I loved her, Zach. I would have given Maxine the world. I can't believe she cheated on me. My wife straight disrespected me. She had this dude putting money in my church." Eli poked himself in the chest. "My church."

Zachariah remained silent. Eli was finally talking. Zach didn't want to hinder his friend from purging the hurt he felt.

"I prayed, Zach. I asked God if this was the woman for me. He kept showing me, Maxine was the woman He chose for me. I even had a random man come up to me after service at Pastor Scott's church. He told me God said Maxine was my wife. Well, he didn't say her name, but he said the woman you are seeing. She was the only woman I was dating."

Interrupting, Zachariah held up his hands. "Look, I'm not saying what this random man said wasn't true, but I will say people tend to lie on God... a lot. I'll bet God is up in heaven shaking his head and telling the angels, 'Look, there they go lying on me again.'"

"Man, be serious. This is my life we're talking about."

"I am being serious. I'm not saying God didn't show you, or say Maxine was supposed to be your wife. The two of you have done a lot of good together. I'll say this and you can take it how you want. I realize you are hurting. I'm not taking anything away from your feelings. If Maxine is the woman God destined to be your wife, then you should talk to her. Not only talk to her, but you have to forgive her. You can't lead a church with unforgiveness in your heart. It's not good for the ministry. More importantly, it's not good for you."

Eli stood and walked away from Zachariah. "It's easy for you to say forgive her. She didn't cheat on you. You didn't have a man sit in your office and tell you he has your wife trained to do whatever he wants. Do you have any idea how much strength it took for me not to break that joker's neck?"

"I know it took strength. Honestly, I don't think I would have been that strong. That's why you're the pastor, not me." Zachariah placed his hand on Eli's shoulder. "Talk to your wife. Whether the two of you decide to work things out or to part ways, it's between you, her, and God. No matter the decision you make concerning your marriage, the two of you need to settle things. Leaving stuff up in the air isn't fair to either of you or the members of the congregation. Think about what I said." Zachariah looked at his watch. "It's time for me to get home. I'm praying for you, man."

Eli walked his friend to the door and took a seat in the living room. He sat in the place Maxine often chose when she needed solitude. Eli had spent so much time being angry over the past couple of weeks, he hadn't allowed himself to accept the reality of his and Maxine's separation.

The aroma from the scent beads Maxine placed throughout the house tantalized his senses. He missed his wife terribly. Although he'd asked her to leave their home, he thought she would still be nearby. Her moving into the guesthouse would insure it. Eli was upset, but if she was in the guesthouse, he would know she was safe. He would also know she wasn't being put up by Jonathan.

When Maxine first left, Eli tossed and turned all night. He'd gotten so used to having her next to him at bedtime that sleep was fleeting. It wasn't until he received a text from his mother-in-law informing him of Maxine's living arrangement that he could relax.

Moving throughout the house, the rooms felt cold and void. The warmth of Maxine's presence was missing. Eli wrestled with the idea of calling her. He considered Zachariah's words. It wasn't that he couldn't forgive his wife. Eli didn't know if he could trust her. Without trust, he believed there was no marriage.

Fifty

A CRISP BREEZE WHISPERED THROUGH THE TREES, causing the fragile leaves to dance. Some glided to the ground. Maxine sat on the park bench, warming her hands on a cup filled with a caramel latte. She glanced around and inhaled the fresh Saturday afternoon air. The innocent play of the birds and squirrels brought an unexpected serenity.

With quiet anticipation, she awaited her companion. Unsure of how the meeting would go, Maxine requested they meet in a neutral location. Things had been tumultuous enough since she'd left home. The last thing Maxine wanted was a confrontation in hostile territory.

"Hey, Maxine. What's up?"

Maxine jumped, startled by the sudden salutation. "You scared the crap out of me."

"You must have been daydreaming or extremely deep in thought to not see me coming. I literally walked right up to you."

"Come here." Maxine extended her arms and pulled her best friend into a tight embrace. "I missed you so much."

"Don't even try it. You didn't miss me too much. Not with

the way you've been ghosting me lately. You have ignored every call and text I sent you." Rashida folded her arms across her chest. "When I saw your text this morning, I almost gave you the same courtesy you gave me."

"I'm sorry, Rashi. Things have been crazy. I couldn't talk. I didn't text because I wasn't ready to deal with the craziness that has become my life."

Maxine grabbed Rashida by the wrist and pulled her down beside her on the bench. Since reaching out via text message earlier in the day, Maxine looked forward to seeing Rashida. They had been friends for several years. She couldn't imagine anyone knowing her better than Rashida. Maxine always shared her deepest secrets and desires with her best friend. She knew she owed Rashida an explanation.

Taking a sip from her cup, Maxine exhaled before recounting the last two weeks. Maxine tried to be strong, but as she began speaking, she couldn't hold back the tears that swelled in her eyes.

"I can't believe this is happening to me. This is crazy." Maxine paused and allowed her words to linger. "I could see if all this happened when I was seeing Jonathan. I wouldn't be messed up about it, but no. Instead, just when everything was going good with me and Eli, Jonathan pulls this mess. That's alright. Jonathan is going to get his."

Rashida placed her hand on Maxine's shoulder, drawing her attention from her rant. "What exactly do you want?"

"What do you mean? What do I want? I want my husband. I want things to go back to normal. I want to stop sleeping in my mama's cramped little house. I want my church back."

"Girl, listen. Of all the things you named, there's only one that you can possibly do something about right now. That's getting out of your mother's house. The other stuff you want, you can only get it with the help of the Lord."

"The Lord, huh? God ain't thinking about me. If He was, all

this craziness wouldn't have happened. Anyway, how am I supposed to get to God if I can't go back to my church?"

"Did you ever pay attention when Eli was preaching? You don't have to go to a church building to reach God. You can pray to God anywhere, at any time. God will hear your prayers from your car, bedroom, or walking down the street, just as well as if you prayed in church. Church is important, but God is everywhere, not just a building with a cross on it."

Maxine considered Rashida's words. It sounded good, but inwardly, she didn't feel strong enough to seek God alone. With all the jacked up stuff she had done, she was pretty sure she was the last person God wanted to hear from. Closing her eyes, Maxine shook her head.

"What you're saying sounds good. It really does. I'm sure there are people that can go straight to God. I'm not that person. If I'm going to get it, it's going to be in church. At least it would have been in a church, but you and I both know I can't show my face at What a Mighty God Cathedral. Those people would run me out of there."

"If you don't feel comfortable going to your church, why don't you go to Alvin's church? The members of his congregation don't know you."

"Yeah, but Alvin knows me. I'm not trying to be judged by your man."

"Alvin is not like that. Shoot, go sit in the back, no big deal. Just go. Tomorrow is as good a time as any."

"If his church is so good, why don't you go there?"

"It's not time for me to attend there yet. Trust me, when the time comes, I have no problem moving my membership. For now, I need to stay at your church. If the people see me leave, knowing I'm your best friend, they will definitely think it's over between you and Eli."

"It is over between us."

"I don't think it is, only God knows. All I know is, you two love each other. Anything can happen. Right now, I'm staying put."

Maxine considered Rashida's words. She was aware of the location of Alvin's church, but Maxine didn't think she could bring herself to attend. She hoped redemption was possible for her, but she couldn't make herself believe it.

Rashida stood and pulled Maxine up next to her. "I know exactly what you need."

"What's that?"

"You need to have some fun. Come on, let's go. I'm going to help take your mind off Eli and the church."

Maxine followed Rashida to the parking lot, where their vehicles sat side by side. "Where are we going?"

"We're going to the rink."

Maxine's eyes widened. "Skating? Oh, no. I haven't skated in years. I'm going to bust my butt."

"If you do, I'm telling you now, I'm going to crack up. Now come on. After we leave the rink, we can get some popcorn from Garrett's."

Clapping her hands, Maxine squealed in delight. "Now you're talking. Garrett's will brighten anybody's mood. Let's go."

Fifty-One

MAXINE HELD HER CELL PHONE SO TIGHT, HER HANDS turned red. She stared at the screen with uncertainty and disbelief. Maxine hadn't seen or spoken to her husband in over a month, and now he was calling her. What could he possibly want? Could he be calling to apologize? The temptation to let the call go to voicemail lingered. As the last ring sounded, she pressed *Accept*.

"Hello," she answered. Her voice was riddled with caution.

"Hello, sweetheart. How are you? You sound good."

"Sweetheart? Eli, I haven't talked to you in over a month. You call out of the blue and have the nerve to address me as sweetheart. Are you serious?" Maxine switched the phone to her other ear. Her irritation showed. "Why are you calling? I don't have time for foolishness."

"Maxine, wait. Please don't hang up. I get it. You're upset. You have every right to be. I'm calling because I miss you. I thought maybe we could get together to talk."

"Talk about what? You didn't seem to want to talk when everything went down. I begged you to talk to me. Instead, you walked away and demanded I leave our home. At this point, I feel like talking to you would be a waste of time."

"I deserve that. Believe me, I'm not trying to dismiss your feelings. I'm man enough to admit I didn't handle things the best way. I got caught up in the heat of the moment. In one conversation, everything I knew to be true about my marriage and ministry came crashing down. What would you have done had you been in my position?"

Maxine softened. She knew she needed to be fair to her husband. She'd deceived him. Eli was giving her the opportunity to talk things out. Hadn't she prayed for this? Maxine knew she owed it to her husband and herself to have the conversation.

"When do you want to meet?"

"Will you come to the house? I want us to speak freely without fear of being overheard or interrupted."

"Yeah. I guess I can meet you there. What time will you be home?"

"I'm here now and will be for the rest of the day."

"Fine, I'll see you in a little while." Maxine prepared to end the call but stopped. "Eli."

"Yes, sweetheart." Eli cleared his throat. "I mean, Maxine."

"Before I get there, I need you to know things between me and Jonathan ended a long time ago. I knew about the money for the carnival, but I did not know he was making the other donation. Jonathan is a man who hates to lose. Money means nothing to him. He uses it as a tool to get what he wants. He is vindictive and manipulative. Since I refused to see him or return his calls, he hit us where he knew he could hurt us both. At the church. Please, believe me."

"Thank you." Eli paused for so long, Maxine thought the call had disconnected. "For what it's worth, I believe you. Drive carefully. I'll see you soon."

Placing her phone next to her on the bed, Maxine reflected on her call with Eli. Had she not been attending Alvin's church, she knew she wouldn't have been able to have such a civil conversation with her husband.

Initially, Maxine was hesitant about attending the church, but with Rashida's prompting, she went. The warmth she felt among the congregation was like nothing she had ever experienced. There was nothing appealing about the storefront location. No fancy décor, widespread community programs, glitz, or glamour. Just a small congregation of people showing the love of Christ.

In the end, it wasn't the welcoming environment that made the difference to Maxine. It was the life-giving message Pastor Adams preached. He spoke of the unconditional love of God in a way she'd never heard before. Maxine pulled the words into her heart. For the first time in her life, Maxine believed she mattered to God. She realized she was not unworthy of God's love and forgiveness.

On the drive home from church, Maxine asked God to forgive her and invited Him into her life. She asked God to heal her heart and to repair her marriage. Maxine knew reconciliation would take a willingness from both her and Eli. She accepted the possibility of them not getting back together. Eli's phone call gave Maxine a huge faith boost. No matter the outcome, his call alone was proof God heard her prayers.

Maxine arrived at the house and rang the doorbell. She still had her key and could have let herself in, but she didn't want to be presumptive. If she tried her key and found Eli had changed the locks, she would have been devastated.

Eli answered the door wearing black slacks and the maroon dress shirt he wore the first time Maxine accompanied him to church. He extended his arms, and Maxine stepped into his embrace. Eli's touch was comforting, like a cashmere blanket on a cool day. He took a deep breath, inhaling the essence of her hair.

"Come on in," he said, allowing her room to enter.

"Thank you." Maxine sashayed inside. The fragrance she wore trailed behind, leaving the scent of vanilla lingering in the air.

"Is it a coincidence you wore the dress I declared my favorite?" Eli took Maxine by the arm and turned her around, taking in a full view of her strapless hot pink body-con dress. The fabric hugged every curve she had. The split on the left exposed her toned thigh. "I remember you purchased this dress in Las Vegas the day after you became my wife."

With her hand in his, Eli walked Maxine into the living room. The sound of soulful ballads filled the room.

"Would you like something to drink?" Eli asked, holding two crystal flutes.

Maxine shook her head. "Thank you, but I'm fine. I came over here because you said you wanted to talk. I'm here now, so let's talk."

"You're right." Eli took a seat next to Maxine on the couch. They turned toward each other, causing their knees to touch. "Let's talk."

"Eli, I know I hurt you. I'm sorry. I was wrong and there is no justification for my actions. You didn't deserve the way I treated you. If I could take it back, I would do so in a heartbeat. Unfortunately, you and I both know it's impossible. I was under so much stress. I took things out on the church staff and you. Once I took time to think about it, I felt horrible. I'm not sure if you're aware, but last week I met with the church leaders and apologized for the way I treated them. I don't know what you want to do concerning our marriage. I've had a long time to think over the past month and I've decided."

"Wait, Maxine, please," Eli interrupted. "Before you go any further. I have something I would like to say. When you and I started dating, I felt like the luckiest man alive. Here I was, a regular guy, nothing special in anyone's eyes. Suddenly, a woman more beautiful than any woman I've ever seen was showing interest in me. At first, I thought it was too good to be true. I knew your interest wasn't based on my financial standing because you were unaware of my financial status. I keep my personal life guarded, so I convinced myself there was no way your interest was based on money."

Maxine attempted to interrupt. Eli raised his hand, stopping her.

"Please, let me finish. With all that we've been through, and all I have revealed, I still believe your interest in me is not financial. Before I met you, I prayed and asked God to send me the woman He desired to be my companion. He sent you. Our lives seemed so different. Here I was, a minister deeply involved in the church, and you didn't attend church at all. So many times, circumstances dictated we should part ways, but there was always something worth staying for."

Eli grabbed Maxine's hands and took them into his own. "You encouraged me to step out and fulfill my dream, and what I believe to be my calling as a pastor. When we started the church, there was so much work involved. With my responsibilities at the dealership, there was no way I could have gotten it all done. But you, the woman God sent me, made it happen. Without you, there's no way What a Mighty God Cathedral would be what it is today. Your presence is missed here and at the church."

"Of all the things I learned about you since we've been together, one thing always stood out to me. The more I tried to love you, the more uncomfortable you appeared to be. One day, to my surprise, things changed. You reciprocated the affection I gave. Our relationship reached a new level. Every moment you've been away from me, I felt like the greatest part of me was missing. From the beginning, and even now, I've wanted to be the man to show you what it means to be loved."

Eli picked up his phone and pressed the key to change the

song playing throughout the room. He stood and pulled Maxine up beside him. "Mrs. Maxine Clayton, may I have this dance?"

The sound of Gerald Levert's *Made to Love You* filled the room. Tears streamed from Maxine's eyes. As the tears fell, Eli kissed them away. "Sweetheart, I forgive you for the things I know about, and any that I don't. In return, I ask you to please forgive me as well. Yes, I'm called by God to be a pastor, but before the church, I'm called to be your husband. Will you allow me to love you the way you deserve to be loved, and continue this journey with me as my wife?"

"Yes, I will, baby. On one condition. You must also be open to me loving you."

Eli pulled Maxine closer and kissed her deeply. "It's time for you to come home."

Maxine wrapped her arms around Eli and whispered in his ear, "I already have."

The Lord has appeared to him from afar, saying:
Indeed, I have loved you with an everlasting love;
therefore with lovingkindness I have drawn you.
Jeremiah 31:3 Holy Bible - Modern English Version

Note from the Author

Thank you for taking the time to read Sedulous: Book Three in the First Lady Series. This book was a labor of love. I thank and praise God for the desire and ability to write stories that show His love. It is my prayer that the stories I write will show God's redemptive power and that every reader will take something away from these stories that will bless your lives.

Whether this is the first book you have read written by me or if you're an avid reader of my books, I want you to know you are loved and appreciated. My daily prayer is that the books I write will touch you in some way, be it entertainment or ministry. Your support does not go unnoticed, and it is very much appreciated.

Once again, I want to thank you for reading Sedulous, I hope you enjoyed it.

If you did and would like to help support the series, the best thing you can do is leave a review at Amazon, Goodreads, online bookseller, or even your personal blog — reviews help other readers determine if a series is to their liking and authors, rely on such word of mouth to get our books in front of new readers.

Your Personal Invitation

Behold, I stand at the door and knock. If anyone hears My voice and opens the door, I will come in to him and dine with him, and he with Me. Romans 3:20 NKJV

As we go through life, we often seek ways to fill void areas in our hearts. Whatever you may be seeking, you can find it in a personal relationship with Jesus Christ.

If you believe God is knocking on the door of your heart, this is your opportunity to welcome Him into your life.

If you have never accepted Jesus Christ as your personal Lord, and Savior, I extend to you this invitation.

About the Author

LaCricia A'ngelle is a licensed Evangelist, Author, and Publisher. She is a wife, mother, and grandmother. Writing has been a part of LaCricia's life since she was a young girl and her passion for the art continues to grow.

To arrange signings, book events, speaking engagements, or to send comments to the author please email her at:
author@lacriciaangelle.com

Connect with LaCricia A'ngelle online at:
http://www.lacriciaangelle.com
Facebook.com/lacriciawrites
Twitter.com/authorlacricia
Instagram.com/lacricia_angelle
TikTok.com/authorlacricia

Acknowledgments

First and Foremost, I give glory and praise to the Most High God. Without Him, none of this would be possible, for I am His Pen. I write the stories He gives me. Stories I pray will honor and glorify Him and draw others to Him.

Special thanks to my husband, Derwin. I went through a lot before you came into my life, but I'm so glad God gave me you. You have been a blessing far beyond my imagination. Literally more than I could ask for. I thank God for your love and encouragement in my writing and life as a whole. Thank you for your prayers and constant reminders of who I am.

To my mother Emma. Thank you so much for everything, Mama. You're always in my corner encouraging me and pushing me to be the best in every endeavor. Your love and support has carried me from my first book Girl, Naw! until now. I love you.

To each of my beautiful children, Keshonna (Xavier), Larry (DeNajae), Gabrielle, Samantha, and my bonus daughter, Ayonna. I love y'all so much and I am honored to be your mother. You all keep me going. My wonderful grandchildren Landon, Carmello, Jayda, Kayleigh, and Josiah. You have my heart and you know it. Always follow your dreams and know that With God all things are possible.

To my mother in love Frances. Our conversations have given me some great content ideas. Thank you for your prayers and the laughter.

To my sisters, nieces, nephews, and the rest of my family. I love you all.

Last but certainly not least, to my readers. Thank you!

My prayer is that my life will encourage others to live their dreams. If God has placed something on your heart to do, do it. As long as you have breath, you have time.

Blessings,

LaCricia A'ngelle

www.ingramcontent.com/pod-product-compliance
Lightning Source LLC
LaVergne TN
LVHW091040080826
845145LV00002B/562